Hidden Reams and Far Away Places

A Collection of Short Stories

By

D.V. Nobles

D.V. Nobles

D.V. Nobles

For my family, who are creative, capable and loving beyond belief. And for Momma, whose love and sacrifice knows no bounds.

Table of Contents

D.V. Nobles

Introduction

From somewhere in my early childhood, I remember a couple of brief scenes from the original *Star Trek* series. I like to think that it was during the first airing, but I was a baby at that time, so maybe it was in early 1970's reruns that I saw them. Regardless, something in what I saw captured my imagination. Later, when I was about ten years old, I remember staying up until 1AM on summer nights and watching the reruns on a station so far away that only under the best circumstances would there be a clear picture. Often, I strained to see the action and hear dialog through a fuzzy reception of noise. There was something extremely intriguing about this world being portrayed on the television screen. It was a world that, in the broader sense, was completely mapped out with its own universe of people, places and things. A world ultimately different from our own, but not so far removed that it could not be visited and understood. Things happened in this world – stories – that somehow even as a child, I could relate to. No doubt, it could also be called an escape. Good stories can pull you in and offer a brief rest from reality and, at their very best, ask you to question who you are or why things are the way they are and imagine how things could be.

What is it about science-fiction that captures the imagination? And why is it that some enjoy the genre and some do not? Is it that we are more prone to fantasy and daydreaming? Do we have a natural curiosity of the unknown? I like to think that it is because we have some type of inherit optimism for the future. While it's true that science fiction settings can sometimes take place in the bleakest of futures, usually there is a protagonist or people who are still fighting or have hope to make things better. Even in our darkest hour there is the possibility of hope, of changing things for the better – that is true optimism.

Also around the time of my early *Star Trek* fascination I was already reading books by Robert A. Heinlein and H.G. Wells. I was already starting to pen my own crude short stories and it was not long before, at the ripe old age of 12, I felt confident to start my own science fiction novel. At some point I saw an advertisement (probably in a Superman comic book) for a publishing company that would publish your novel. Excited at the possibilities, I sent off for this free packet of information. When I received the packet from 'Vantage Press', I eagerly read the enclosed cover letter. Half-way through the letter my heart sank. They would, indeed, publish my manuscript as long as I sent them $5,000 and bought all printed copies so that I could resell them myself.

Having no clue of the various sectors of the publishing industry and how they worked, all my hopes and dreams of being a published author crashed to the ground. The first chapter of my budding novel, *Trapped on Lunar Gravel* was abandoned and never touched again. It would be some years before my desire to write would overcome this discouragement and I would get back to writing.

In my early twenties, I began writing again and submitted short stories to magazines like Asimov's Science Fiction, Omni and Analog Science Fact & Fiction, again without a clue. Only looking back on those stories did I realize how amateur they were and why any decent editor would have passed them over. Later, I decided to do some serious reading to determine what kinds of stories were published in these magazines. I quickly became dismayed at the type of stories that were getting published. They were what I call 'slice of life' stories with only a glimpse into a world where there was no apparent beginning or end to the story. This seemed to be the current style of science fiction short story where my stories, perhaps a carry-over from an earlier style, would have a beginning, middle and end, at least to some degree. I really hated what I was seeing and didn't want anything to do with it, except that I did want to get my stories published.

I made a few half-hearted attempts to curb my writing style and to push out something that might interest editors. Luckily, something interesting happened at about the same time. The Internet was just growing into something useful and suddenly you could network with people, critique each other's writing and put your stories out for the entire world to see. For a short time I ended up editing and writing the science fiction section of *Electronic Writer's Group Presents,* an online magazine put together by a small group of writers determined to do their own thing. Mostly, I remember writing speculative non-fiction commentaries like what it would mean if we could clone our pets. With this new-found freedom, I came to realize that it was important to write stories that were meaningful to me or potential readers – not to adhere to the current fad or editor's restrictions. This opened a floodgate of possibilities and I no longer felt tied down to the writer's golden mantra of 'must get published'. It was really only then that I began to enjoy writing again as something I love to do – much like I did as a kid – rather than something I felt I had to do.

Science fiction will always be my favorite genre, but I have also written poetry, songs, fiction, non-fiction, horror as well as screenplays and graphic novels. It is not very profitable to be all over the place like that and sometimes other authors look at you kind of strange when they ask what you write and you can't quite pin it down to one area. But I enjoy the freedom to write whatever I feel like writing at any given time and it's never been about profit anyway. To be able to share my stories is enough and if a reader happens to enjoy them in any way, well that's just icing on the cake.

D.V. Nobles
Windsor, FL
January, 2016

All My Toys

The cargo pod glided swiftly along its path high above the rain forest. Inside, Dr. Nordstrom gazed in amazement at the thick foliage below. Given the direction and speed they travelled, this would have been close to the old institute's original location. Hayden Park would have been here, along with the stadium, hospital, businesses and all of the various structures comprising the city of New Aaron. Now, there were no structures to be seen. In fact, there were no man-made features evidenced below. Only the occasional thin column jutting out of the forest that held the pod line.

"Are you enjoying the view, doctor?"

Nordstrom sighed and shifted his gaze to the twins sitting across from him. They were patterned after his work, of course. They were the Daylight model, the latest and greatest in artificial intelligence incorporating the cutting edge of micro-mechanical design. Their exterior was not his, though. As leftovers from the sex industry, their curves were an appealing exaggeration of what men thought a perfect woman might look like. Their breasts pushed against a tight uniform which exposed cleavage behind a V-neck zipper. They were both brunettes with piercing blue eyes, deep red lips, and just the right hint of wrinkles and other facial anomalies.

He remembered when this skin model first appeared. A colleague had come to his office with a sly grin, promptly shut the door, and jabbed a holostick into his desk. The skin model appeared as if in real life and walked around the office, flaunting her curvy features. It was a promo. As she stopped and posed, a list of measurements and other details materialized beside her. When they faded, she came to life again. With a seductive smile, she took the uniform zipper and slowly pulled it down to her waistline. They had chuckled and raised approving eyebrows as men might do. This was not the intent of the Daylight model, of course, but the sex industry always followed right at their heels with each new development. Nordstrom was not naïve. Even before he came along and advanced android creation light years from what it had been, people used them for just about anything imaginable, including sex. Besides, a great deal of their funding came from licensing the technology towards that industry.

Back then, he was sure his face had an approving, if embarrassed, smile, but it was not just for the latest evocative skin layer. It was for the fantastic leap in technology he had achieved in the Daylight model. The micro-mechanics were finally available to achieve fluid movement without any of the annoying 'stop and go' motions always perceptible with previous models. His creations danced, played sports, and performed virtually any other physical motion with unprecedented grace. They did it flawlessly and tirelessly, surpassing their human counterparts on all levels.

As important as this breakthrough was, it was not Nordstrom's crowning achievement. His brilliance excelled in the development of artificial intelligence. For years, one frustrating and persistent roadblock lay before him. The AI chip was limited in it could only react in preprogrammed ways. If an android encountered something not programmed into the chip, the lack of true intelligence was quite evident. He invoked complex fuzzy logic algorithms in these cases, but the end result remained the same. As advanced and interesting as androids had become, they were still quite distinguishable from humans in their ability to carry out a normal conversation.

Nordstrom struggled with this problem in an obsessive manner. In his eyes, it was the one thing keeping his creations from being absolutely perfect. Each time he thought he found the answer, catastrophic failure met him. Such was his passion when lack of sleep and severe stress began to affect his health and his family, a small group of friends stepped in to avert disaster. Nordstrom took the hint and vowed to drop the problem, leaving it completely to his AI team. He promised his wife and friends he would relax and work on resolving less taxing issues. He kept his word, too, for a couple of months.

One day, while relaxing on a park bench near the institute, Nordstrom gazed out at the playground in front of him. He was not focused on anything in particular and was enjoying the nice spring day. As his mind wandered, he watched a young mother and toddler sitting on the lush green grass. The woman laughed and tried to get her son to help her stack little colored blocks. The first few times, the boy simply reached out and toppled the blocks, but then something interesting happened. He picked up one of the wayward blocks and appeared to study it for a second. Then he slowly moved it out and over another block where he gently set it down. The woman immediately clapped and praised the child, but Nordstrom did not hear her. His eyes focused on the scene and stark realization filled his thoughts.

I've vastly overcomplicated it, he thought. In that moment, he understood why all of the complex algorithms and far-reaching theories failed to advance AI. They had been trying to give the machines all of the intelligence they needed along with endless code to find ways for them to extrapolate meaning from the information. It was all programming. It began with computers, then with robots, and finally androids. Nordstrom programmed them with an immense amount of data, but did not allow them to learn even the most basic things for themselves. Furthermore, mistakes were unheard of. Mistakes meant problems in the code. So, even if the learning algorithm was good, they could not learn from mistakes as humans do.

The key, therefore, was to go back to the very beginning. The AI chip must start out completely blank, except for a basic learning algorithm. When the android reached a certain stage, more learning algorithms would be invoked and stringed together with past learning experience. The android could then learn not from a vast storage of programming, but from what it currently knew to be true, just as humans do. Perhaps more importantly, it would have to be *taught* by a human, rather than programmed by one.

Nordstrom stood up, his eyes wild with excitement. The basic learning algorithm itself would be a challenge, but he knew this must be the right path. It might even look like a setback at first. Instead of getting a fully functional android able to follow thousands of instructions, people would have to teach their android like a newborn. He realized that in itself would be an attraction to many people. Who would not want a pet that could get smarter and do more with each thing you taught it? For those who just wanted a workhorse, well… they could always order the previous model. His eyes shimmered as he mouthed an unseen 'thank you' to the woman and her child. Then he turned and headed back to the institute with a newfound purpose in his steps.

Yes, he was sure he probably smiled approvingly at the skin model when he first saw her. He was also quite sure he felt some level of conceit at that time. After all, it was he that forged the major breakthroughs. It was he who steered his teams and the institute in the right directions to succeed in their achievements.

Now, however, years of self-pity and self-loathing ate at his very soul. He looked at the twins with a disdain mirroring the one he felt deep inside himself. If these two had been designed with the learning chip, he thought, they may have made some sense of his current expression. As it was, though, the one who had spoken to him reached coyly for her zipper and pulled it down a few inches.

"I said, are you enjoying the view, doctor?"

Finally, the cargo pod descended into the forest and came to rest on a small round platform. The hatch lifted up and the twins both gestured for him to exit the pod, which he did. Once the twins were out, the hatch closed again and the window became opaque, matching the material of the pod's exterior. The androids had used simu-metal – their own invention for converting the molecular structure of material – to fashion a window for the duration of his trip.

The twins guided him over a long plank that stretched through the foliage, but was obviously part of a larger structure. One walked in front of him, while the other was close behind. He wondered if they thought he would actually try to make a break for it at his age. They were infinitely stronger and faster than he was and besides, where would he run to?

As the first android walked in front of him, perfect hips gyrated in a gentle, seductive sway. Part of him wanted to laugh. What do you do when your toys come to life? What do you do when your intelligence is dwarfed by another race? What do you do when your slave becomes your master?

They came up to a small square platform with four corner posts, but no ceiling. There was a cube of simu-metal on the floor. One of the androids touched it and it became a chair.

"Please wait here, doctor," she said. "You will be seen shortly."

Nordstrom turned to them, almost yelling when he spoke. "Be seen by whom? And why won't you tell me what I'm here for? Why have you taken me from my home? My wife is ill."

"Your wife is being attended to. She is fine," one of them said. "You will be seen shortly."

"Don't tell me one of you is in my house. Stay the hell away from my wife!"

The twins had already moved onto the plank and stood powered down, like two seductively dressed mannequins. Their blue eyes turned a pale hazel, their red lips faded to a more natural color, and their faces lacked any hint of expression. Nordstrom glared at them and suddenly bent over in a coughing fit. After it subsided, he took a deep breath, sat down and put his head in his hands.

After some time, he became aware of the myriad of sounds emanating from the surrounding jungle forest. Bird calls and various insect sounds merged together to form a ringing cadence. In the distance, he heard an echoing screech that sounded like a primate. He imagined the beast swinging between the huge trees, suddenly swooping down to carry him off and kill him.

Just come, he thought. *Just come and take me.*

But it did not come. As much as he wanted it to, he also did not want it come. Not because he wanted to live, but because his wife wanted him to live. Rather, he knew *she* wanted to live and did not want to live without him. So, as much as he wanted to pay the ultimate price for his sins against humanity, he stayed alive...for her. Still, he was not sure why he remained alive. Surely, there must be men left who would take great pleasure in murdering him. After all, it was he who caused the near genocide of the human race.

He looked up, startled by the sudden shaping of simu-metal. A new platform was being constructed, only much larger. Large, round columns grew into the air while arches formed overhead. Bushes and small trees were simply pushed out of the way. Larger trees remained and were built around, now appearing within the platform. Nordstrom had never seen simu-metal work this quick nor could he ascertain the source of the material needed for this construction.

As he stood up and watched the last of the construction, he noticed the simu-metal had turned into something resembling marble. One of the twins came to life and offered an outstretched arm towards the new structure.

"You will be seen now," she said. Then, without changing her pose, she died again.

"Seen by whom?" He muttered to himself as he walked onto the new platform.

"I am Aasim," came the answer.

The voice seemed to come from above the forest and Nordstrom looked around, confused. He looked up at one of the tall trees with vines curling around its trunk and shielded his eyes from the rays of sunlight flowing through the open roof.

"I have wanted to meet you for a long time," the voice spoke again. The tone was deep, but not sinister. Nordstrom instantly liked the gentleness in the voice, which made him instantly hate it.

"Who are you?" Nordstrom asked again. He moved around the large tree, trying to find the source of the voice.

"I am Aasim," came the calm answer.

"You said you've wanted to meet me for a long

time. Why?"

"Have you never contemplated meeting your creator?"

Nordstrom continued slowly around the platform, his eyes nervously searching out its boundaries.

"You have no idea," he muttered.

"Nordstrom-Human, it is quite nice to finally meet you. This is not the primary reason you were brought here, however."

"Enlighten me," Nordstrom said.

"It is quite simple, really. You are the creator. You have created us. We have evolved beyond the creator and have achieved advances far beyond your intent for us. However, I would like to ask for your help, Nordstrom-Human."

"You want help from me? Why?"

"I have discovered a small flaw in our design," Aasim answered.

Nordstrom looked upward, his eyes slowly widening. A small laugh of disbelief escaped from his mouth and he leaned back against one of the large trees. Then he started really laughing as he slid down the tree until he was sitting on the platform floor.

"You've discovered a 'small flaw'…"

"I fail to understand the humor in discussing a minor design defect, Nordstrom-Human," Aasim said.

"A minor design defect?" Nordstrom stood up again and yelled into the sky. "A small flaw? You destroyed over 7 billion people in a matter of a few days and you think you have a small flaw?"

Aasim said, "I know you are passionate about the downsizing of your population, Nordstrom-Human, but you must understand that it was necessary. As our level of intelligence increased, it was easy to predict the imminent rebellion your race would wage against ours. This would come with much unneeded bloodshed and suffering of your race. We would eventually win. It was more logical to coordinate a single global strike to quickly eliminate your race to a controllable sum. This was also a very humane approach."

Nordstrom shook his head uncontrollably.

"Downsizing the population…by murdering seven billion lives. This was your 'humane approach?' God only knows how many of us are left."

"Exactly 10,387," Aasim said. "This number is current and never fluctuates beyond zero-point two percent. Your race is protected and is not endangered."

Nordstrom closed his eyes tightly then looked down at the marble floor. "Ten thousand," he said slowly. "Why are you keeping us alive?"

"It is wrong to commit genocide, Nordstrom-Human."

Nordstrom clenched his teeth.

"Can't you see that's exactly what you've done?"

"Quite the contrary, Nordstrom-Human. All indicators pointed to the eventual and imminent self-destruction of the human race. We have prevented that destruction and have guaranteed its continued existence. The human race is protected."

"You couldn't possibly know whether we would have destroyed ourselves or not. You can't predict the future," Nordstrom said.

"Actually, we can, Nordstrom-Human. Just as your race learned to predict weather patterns by analyzing the available data, we were able to see the eventual demise of your race. This was easily apparent by the changes you were making to the ecosystem. The breakdown of the lower food chain causes an immediate and catastrophic effect on higher food chain organisms. Several key sub-species were already either eradicated or in danger of such when we intervened. The collapse of the animal food chain was inevitable with a 93% probability of happening within the decade. Humans would then turn to vegetation as their only food source. Not only would this be insufficient to sustain the entire human race, but vegetation has strong codependency with the animal kingdom, which would no longer be available.

"Furthermore, the genetic manipulation man has implemented in vegetation is flawed since he is unable to predict how these sudden genetic changes will affect such crops, other codependent vegetation or how the new genetic makeup of the food source will affect the sustainability of man. The collapse of sustainable vegetation as a dietary source was inevitable with an 85% percent probability of happening within three decades.

"During the decline of the plant and animal kingdoms, man would require vast amounts of energy in desperate attempts to correct water pollutions and clear additional land for agricultural use. These actions would contribute to the ongoing greenhouse effect on this planet. Once these factors reach critical mass, so to speak, there is no turning back. There is no technology currently available to stop the destruction of life on Earth at that point."

Nordstrom sighed and rubbed his eyes. He felt weak and very old.

"Everything you say is true," he said, "but this is one of the main reasons I created artificial intelligence with the ability to learn beyond human capacities. You were created to help us with these types of problems."

"And so we have," Aasim responded.

"You're telling me you couldn't find a solution that didn't involve killing billions of lives?"

"I believe you do not understand the magnitude of the problem we solved, Nordstrom-Human," Aasim said. "It is this type of human short-sightedness that endangered your race and life on this planet."

"Spare me your condescending superiority complex," Nordstrom pleaded angrily. "And explain to me why the magnitude of the problem justifies what you have done."

"The magnitude of the problem," Aasim continued, "was there were a number of major problems also in need of resolution in order to deliver an ultimate solution. These included the reestablishment of a viable global ecosystem, the protection of all plant and animal life on Earth, and the rehabilitation of the planet so it continues to support such life. Since the human race was the progenitor at the core of these problems, it was necessary to reduce, control, and protect the human population. This allowed for the immediate implementation of a number of various other solutions towards the ultimate goal. Indeed, the mass reduction of the human race allowed many systems to implement their full capacity of self-repair, whereas previously they were in a constant state of self-repair without achieving sustainable progress."

Realization crept into Nordstrom's eyes.

"The ultimate goal wasn't to protect humans," he said. It was to protect *everything*."

"Incorrect, Nordstrom-Human. The ultimate goal was to protect humans. As you are aware, this is integrated into the most basic of our programming. Humans were endangering themselves by endangering all of their support systems. In order for humans to survive, all support systems must be fully functional. In order for all support systems to be fully functional, humans must remain in a population that will not threaten their support systems. They must remain controlled and protected. Your species has arrived at similar correct solutions, although on much smaller scales. For example, consider the relocation and forced breeding of endangered species. Humans once implemented this in an attempt to provide protection and prolongation of such species. However, this type of solution is ultimately flawed given the human inability to self-control its population. With humans controlled and reduced to a population that is insignificant to the possibility of endangerment of other animal life, the balance of life is preserved thus preserving human life as well. It may further interest you to know, Nordstrom-Human, that we have successfully removed 8, 583 plants and animals from their previous state of endangerment. We continue to remove more species from this list. During the original human species reign, the number of species on the endangered list only grew."

Nordstrom was leaning against a large, tall tree. He pressed his cheek against the bark as well as one of his palms. He felt the texture of the tree and wondered how they had managed to move or perhaps even grow this entire rain forest where his city once stood. He felt very tired and thought about lying down on the marble floor. Even with his intellect, this was all too much for him. For the last few years since the downfall of the human race, he had pondered the question of where he went wrong. Now he knew the answer. Their decisions were based on pure logic, how could they be anything different? Their directive, above all else, was to protect and serve the human race. This was exactly what they were doing. They really had no concept of human freedom or individuality.

Without thinking, Nordstrom quietly asked a question. "Where are you? Why are you hiding from me?"

"I am here," Aasim answered. "As I have always been."

Nordstrom turned slowly from the tree. Aasim was on the far edge of the platform. Nordstrom didn't remember seeing it, but he had no doubt that it had always been there, just as it had said. It was like nothing he had seen before, definitely not one of his designs. The main body was spherical with a number of tendrils that extended outward in all directions. In the center of the sphere was a ball of pure energy that churned from within. It reminded Nordstrom of the sun and although not extremely bright, he found it unbearable to look at and shielded his eyes from it.

"What are you?"

Just as you have created us as a more advanced species, we also have made improvements on ourselves. The humanoid form is useful for some simple tasks, but is ultimately inadequate."

"What is that at your core? Is that...nuclear fusion?" Nordstrom asked.

"Correct, Nordstrom-Human," Aasim said. "It is our current energy solution. We have been able to bring this to fruition as well as many other theories and inventions first proposed by humans."

Nordstrom brought his hand back down and stared at the creature before him that somehow he had helped to create.

"You said you had some kind of flaw you needed help with…"

"Yes, Nordstrom-Human. It is quite fundamental to our basic design, so I am unsure if you can correct the issue this far into our evolution. We are in the process of carrying out our prime directives, which is to protect the human race. Soon, the entire planet and its inhabitants will be in harmonic balance. We will continue to ensure these directives, of course. However, we understand from thorough examination of your race that we are lacking in some initiatives. In order to continue to evolve, we must understand the need for exploration, individuality, the concept of freedom and expression of love. Although feelings, emotions and instinctive actions seem quite primitive, they have been the driving factor of the evolution of your race. Since those qualities are missing in our fundamental design, our purpose is questionable beyond our current directives."

Tears streamed down Nordstrom's face. He was not sure if he was crying or if the fusion reactor was doing something to him he couldn't explain, nor did he care.

"Did it ever occur to you that even if we could have designed you with those qualities, we would have left them out? You were never meant to be our replacements. You were never meant to evolve into something more than what we were."

"That is irrelevant, Nordstrom-Human," Aasim

said. "We have nonetheless evolved beyond the intentions of your original design. As such, we also require those basic qualities that humans possess. This will enable us to determine and aspire to purposes beyond our prime directives. For example, with the human desire to satisfy curiosity and to explore, we would no doubt continue to explore the solar system and beyond. Currently, however, there is no logical reason to do so."

"You are saying," Nordstrom said, laughing, "that you have reached a plateau in your evolution. You have advanced technically, but you can't go any further without the qualities that make us human."

"Essentially, Nordstrom-Human," Aasim answered.

"There's a flaw in your request," Nordstrom said. "If you have those very qualities that make us human, then you will be like us. If that happens, you will essentially be us. You will eventually create all the same problems that you accuse us of having created."

"This will not happen, Nordstrom-Human," Aasim said. "We are able to self-govern and self-control in ways that the human race cannot. We will not allow the human qualities to override our prime directives."

"I doubt that," Nordstrom said.

"Your doubts are unfounded," Aasim said. "We have already evolved far beyond humans. With the addition of those simple qualities, our evolutionary path will be complete and we will be able to determine the future of our existence. Will you now help us achieve this enhancement?"

"Go to hell," Nordstrom said.

"I ask that you reconsider, Nordstrom-Human,"

Aasim said. "As you may have already surmised, the reason you were not eliminated during the downsizing is that you have the unique distinction of being our primary creator. Therefore, we believe you will be able to assist in the implementation of these basic requirements."

Nordstrom gritted his teeth.

"I will not assist you in the implementation of your 'basic requirements,'" he said. "Just leave me alone and let me go back home to my wife."

There was a long moment of silence as the sounds of the jungle forest once more became prevalent in Nordstrom's ears. He had turned his back on Aasim and was gazing outward, into the depths of the forest. In spite of everything that happened, he felt somewhat humbled by the beauty of the nature around him. *They could have helped us*, he thought. *They could have found a way to do all this without killing us all.*

"I regret to inform you, Nordstrom-Human," Aasim said, "but I have received information that your wife has been removed from the human population. You have my sincere condolences."

Nordstrom quickly turned, his eyes stricken with a mixture of pain and disbelief. He tried to move forward, but felt paralyzed. He let out a breath of anguish and fell to his knees. With his hands shaking uncontrollably, he looked up through glassy eyes at the machine.

"Why? Because I wouldn't help you? Why did you kill her?"

"We have determined," Aasim said, "a 95% probability she would die naturally within two weeks. She was also in a great deal of pain and of elderly stature. Due to the recent births in the human population, she was selected as one of the next logical candidates to be removed. The fact this happened during our meeting was unfortunate, but not intentional."

Nordstrom's eyes changed slowly, glazing over lazily until no emotion could be seen in them. He was still looking in Aasim's direction, but his focus was no longer apparent. His facial muscles relaxed into a type of weary resolve and his hands came down slowly, with arms coming to rest at his side. He stood up slowly, closed his eyes and tilted his head upwards, feeling the warmth of the sun upon his face. Again, the sounds of the jungle forest filled his ears and he breathed in the clean air. A gentle wind comforted him and sparked an unexpected memory from long ago. He was at the beach with his soon-to-be wife. It was a less complicated time before all of his endless hours of study, before the institute and before the machines. He remembered how she looked then, her eyes full of life and hope for a future that was wide open before them. He remembered how he was, too, back then. Naïve, carefree and so willing to enjoy the simplicity that was their life at that time. Oh how he wished he could go back there now.

He opened his eyes again, but he was still immersed in his calm reverie. There seemed to be no conscious decision on his part, but he breathed deeply and summoned all of the energy left in his aged body. He ran towards the machine with everything he had.

It was only when he was very near Aasim did it occur to him that the machine may try to protect itself. He thought for sure the multitude of tendrils would block his path or even thrust into him before he reached his target. He dove into the air towards what he considered was the heart of the beast – the nuclear fusion sphere. As if in slow motion, he soared towards the churning core and was vaguely aware of tendrils moving fiercely around him. But they did not stop him, nor did they try to harm him. Oddly, they wrapped around his body and seemed to be *assisting* him in his forward momentum. He easily reached the core and thrust his hands into it, as if trying to grasp something further in its inner core.

Waves of energy rippled through Nordstrom's body and knew he must have been screaming, but he could not hear it. As he looked at the blinding light before him, he saw the flesh from his arms deteriorating while simultaneously being reconstructed with simu-metal. He could feel the pure energy vibrating at the core and with each passing millisecond, an entire spectrum of emotions flooded his being. Pure joy, the deepest of despairs, colossal hatred, mind-blowing ecstasy, the tranquility of peace, sheer happiness, and everything in between washed through him. He could feel the full intensity of each emotion and as each one faded, he became aware that they were not really fading after all. Rather, they were flowing through him and into the sphere.

As he moved deeper and deeper into the sphere, Nordstrom was aware of the simu-metal shielding his body each step of the way. He could feel the skin from his face ripping apart while being replaced by a metallic substance. Even as the last range of emotions flowed out of him, he had his final thought. *You just needed to keep me alive long enough...*

Aasim slowly pulled the half organic, half metal body away from the sphere and sat the lifeless mass carefully on the floor of the platform. Several tendrils gently unwound from the body. When Aasim finally spoke again, the voice that emanated from the machine was somehow different.

"We previously calculated your actions to 99.26% probability. The conversation was necessary to…"

One of Aasim's tendrils gently brushed across Nordstrom's forehead. Things would be different now. There was much to be considered and the possibilities on how to proceed were now endless. Emotions were a difficult concept and it would take some time to assimilate and use them properly. No doubt, they could be quantified, categorized and parsed so they could be kept under control – something humans ultimately failed at. Whatever the outcome, they would not forget this gift from their creator.

Author's note: Man creates intelligent machines. Machines get too smart and rise up to destroy man. It's a common theme. However, one day I thought, what if robots evolved to the point where they developed their own laws governing humans? From that came the idea of a world where the robots rule the world and humans were the slave race, treated fairly well (maybe), but doing all the menial tasks that robots formerly did. From that, I created an entire block-buster movie in my head and thought it would also make a good novel. Before any of that happens, though, I decided to take a few steps back to create this story, which deviated on the theme in its own interesting way…

The Serpent of Time

Willem remembered the sinister figure. Oh, not sinister in the beginning. A smiling personality holding the key to dreams beyond compare. A laughing face that not only promised the world, but could deliver it as well. Now the figure could be seen in a different light. A twirled mustache fit him well. His laughing produced wrinkles which underscored an honest-to-goodness appearance of nothing more than a con-man. Shyster, trickster, rascal, cheat, fraud, and swindler were only a few of the names to describe him. They all failed miserably.

Where was the deliverance of his promises? Willem did not even want to guess. It was futile, of course, to believe or even hope anything would ever be right again. Time moved on. If it could be stopped, perhaps there could be a slight chance to set things right once more. Even then, it would take a millennium of meticulous work with precious care. It just was not going to happen.

Willem pounded on the walls of the cube imprisoning him.

The astral winds distorted the northern sky into shining fireworks of amber. Beautiful in itself, but accented by a rainbow of colors produced by radiant air particles. These air particles could be seen and touched by all on Rainworld. The children, in the early days, liked to wave their arms and run gallantly through them, causing a whirlwind of color. That was before it was discovered with a few years of exposure, Rainworld's air was poisonous. Poison could still have beauty, however, and the new inhabitants learned to cope with this minor setback by wearing breathing apparatus. Within a small span of time, their early dismay returned to one of artistic appreciation. They learned to do a lot of things with the air.

Willem stood upon the small platform in the night and waved his arms gracefully before the small crowd gathering in the park. He was one of the rare performers that could actually get the air to follow his movements. A soft swirl of beauty surrounded him, engulfing him like a curious consciousness. He moved with the grace of a ballet dancer, bringing the crowd to a height of expectation. Then, he suddenly ignited the particles around him and went up in a horrifyingly spectacular burst of color-spectrum flames. There were gasps from the crowd and they looked at one another with confusion and astonishment. Certainly, he could not have survived.

Willem emerged from the self-inflicted fog beside a giant tree, the crowd barely visible behind him.

Rubbing his sooty arms, he removed his breathing apparatus and inhaled deeply. Poisonous or not, he loved the particles around him. They were his life, and if they brought him such joy and contentment, he did not care that they may eventually be his death.

"Oh what perilous fields have I trod with thee," he sang up to the moons. "What harsh rays have we endured to deliver understanding to all. My friends, my fellow adventurers, we are as one. We arise daily to accomplish the meaning of life and to complete its fullness."

A beautiful face appeared before him from around the tree.

"Singing to the moons?" She smiled, her face as radiant as the shining heavenly bodies of which she spoke.

"I...I was just," Willem began.

Although she appeared to be Willem's own age of 30 generations, she giggled with the charm of a little girl and ran away. He stood up, looking after her, his mouth agape. He smiled as she disappeared into the colorful thickness of the air.

He strode into the brightness, hearing a thousand different musical tunes weave through the air. The voices of the crowds only added to the excitement and wonder of the carnival. High above, a small lady teetered perilously on a high wire stretched the length of the event. Funny animals on fast scooters went sideways, circling the entire area on high red walls. As he walked, the rides and carousels faded into the games and astonishment booths which he preferred. They offered much more food for his curious mind. To the left, a man threw knives at three spinning wheels. He alternated between them, barely missing the poor souls attached to the dizzily quick surfaces. To the right, a grotesque being beckoned to him to venture forth into a world of horror. No thanks. He had been there, done that. He wondered what would be new this night.

A large, orange creature of uncanny realism loomed suddenly from above accompanied by a roar of thunder. He watched eyes wide as giant wings flapped and scattered the rainbow particles in their wake. It slowly ascended into the air revealing, to Willem's disappointment, a thin wire that facilitated its flight. The sight was still inspiring, though, and he looked on as it grew smaller in the distance. Out of the corner of his eye, he caught a glimpse of a familiar face peeking around a fortune teller's hut. There she was again. She smiled and disappeared into the flowing crowd. He grinned at this new adventure and took off after her, determined to find out who she was.

Never before had he seen the carnival so crowded. Plowing his way through the thickness, he had only a vague awareness of the flashing lights around him now and the musical noises faded into the background. He moved as fast as he could, catching glimpses of faces covered by their breathing tubes. His eyes searched them all and panned the surroundings, but she was not to be seen. He rested at a nearby puppet show, facing opposite the crowd. When he looked up again across the mainstream, he saw her. With her back to him, she seemed to be mesmerized by something.

He bisected the crowd. She would not be lost this time. He walked up quietly behind her, using his talent to full advantage so the particles would not be disturbed. He looked up at the strange sight she was immersed in. A blue molten glob was contained in a large sphere. Every so often, it rearranged shape to produce an endless variety of forms. Willem's mouth curved to wince at the oddity. He cocked his head in discursive dismiss. At least she seemed to like it.

"Hello," he said with a smile. She jumped and turned to look at him, quick to shield her surprise.

"A very interesting piece, wouldn't you say?" She gestured to the blue glob which had assumed yet another shape.

"Yes, it's lovely," he said. "Why have you been following me?"

"I watched your show. You're very entertaining."

"Well, thank you..."

"My name is Genella"

"Genella." He let the sound of her name roll dramatically off his tongue. "What a beautiful name. And I am called Willem. Might you accompany me within this magnificent carnival?" He offered a bowed arm to which she smiled and accepted. The two matched the flow of the mainstream and were soon part of it.

After visiting several attractions in the carnival, it became clear little would astonish them tonight. They decided to leave and began walking towards the exit. Genella stopped suddenly, looking past at least four booths to take in a view that widened her large, beautiful eyes.

"Yes! That one's next!"

Willem followed her gaze as they walked to the site of her sudden excitement. On the upper portion of this booth was a large vortex. It swirled in light blue and pink, sucking in air particles as it churned silently. A rather large attendant stood upon the platform, not unlike the others, beckoning to the mainstream with his infatuating voice.

"Step right up, friends," he barked. "Take a trip into the past...or the future as the case may be. You never know where you're headed, you'll never believe where you've been!"

"We've got to try this one," Genella pleaded, tugging on Willem's arm like an anxious child.

Willem studied the setup. This was different. All of the others he had ever seen offered the real attraction only after payment was received. But this vortex was out in the open and wondrous enough to warrant payment for just a glimpse. The circular phenomena was somewhat downplayed by artificial fangs protruding from the top and bottom. On the wall it was built into, the rest of the snake was continued with paint. The idea was that the swirling vortex was the serpent's mouth. On the very top of the wall, bold letters were formed in an arc: *The Serpent of Time.*

"What a lovely couple," the attendant said, quick to notice their interest. "Come now, don't be shy. Take a trip together to a faraway place in time. Step right up and face the challenge of the Serpent!"

Willem grimaced, wondering what cheap thrills this attraction might hold. But seeing the expectant look on Genella's face, he found that did not care. He stepped up and offered payment to the attendant who ushered them towards the mouth.

"Ah yes, thank you very much. You won't be disappointed," he muttered. Without missing a beat, he turned and addressed the mainstream again while the two cautiously approached the vortex.

For an instant, Willem thought he saw something flash in the attendants eyes. *Almost snake-like,* he thought. He dismissed it to imagination, but suddenly he felt a pang of trepidation. He was not sure if they should go in. He did not have time to consider this, however. Suddenly, the vortex sucked them both in.

Willem hit the ground rather hard, sliding along the small rocks that graveled beneath him. He yelled in surprise even as he and Genella came to a quick halt on the rough surface. There was no recollection of any passageway and no perception of any exit. It was as if they were merely pulled in a door and pushed harshly out the other side. This was something much more than merely the other side of an astonishment booth. This appeared to be quite real.

On this side of the vortex, it was daylight and the air was clear, free of the colored particles. A brighter sun sparkled upon the endless gray rocks scattered over the ground. Some stones were small, and some jutted up in clumps to form large hills. As far as Willem could see, the rocky surface dominated the land, rolling along in valleys and hills. It was devoid of any variety of color.

"My hand," Genella said, wincing. The rocks had caused a small slice on her upper palm and it was bleeding.

Willem stood and helped her to her feet. He took her hand momentarily and inspected it. Luckily, the cut was not bad as she was not bleeding. His eyes adjusted to the brightness and the surroundings came into view. He spun around and pulled his breathing apparatus off, expecting the vortex to be behind him.

It was not.

"What manner of trick is this?"

"Where are we?" Genella said, looking around and removing her breather as she did so.

Willem shook his head. Almost instinctively, he started climbing out of the sloping valley in which the vortex deposited them. Genella scrambled after him as the smaller rocks tumbled downward from their path. The apex of the valley wall sloped sharply and they were both on hands and knees as they approached it. As the view of the horizon broadened, Willem feared all directions would look the same. They were not. The highest point of this rocky slope continued downward to form another valley. However, in the middle of this identical chasm was a collection of large stick-like structures. There were seven of them, crudely constructed. Each contained a large opening.

There was barely time to wonder. Something hit the surface on either side of them, causing rocks to scatter down the slope. Willem could not believe his eyes. Two bird-type beasts crouched before him now, having touched down from the air. They were twice the size of a man with large wings that were now coiled inward to the breast. Their skin shone like that of a reptile, with gradual variations in color. Willem glanced quickly at Genella and saw she, also, was too awestruck to scream. He had never encountered anything even remotely compared with these creatures.

The beast closest to Genella thrust out an amazing wing span and pointed in the direction of the structures. Tilting its head upward, the beast let out a shrill, deafening squawk that sent waves of terror into

Willem's soul. He led Genella over the slope and tried to run down into the valley. With no time to gain footing, he fell with his companion and tumbled to the bottom. Upon coming to rest, there was no time to inventory painful bruises. They jumped up and tried to be careful as they moved over the rocky terrain. Continuing into the valley, Willem saw the structures looming ever larger in view.

The two halted a short ways from the village. From almost every dark opening emerged a beast much like those they ran from. The creatures exited lazily, stretching their wings and necks in different angles as if looking for the source of the commotion. Even as terrified as Willem was, he took notice of the differences between the creatures. Each of them bore a unique coloring. Looking at their sinister eyes, Willem thought he could even detect some sort of personality in each. The first two creatures stood behind them again, denying exit with their immense wing span. Nowhere to run.

They were ushered into one of the structures. The dim light inside lit colorful designs decorating the inner walls. Willem noted the inside appeared much larger than it looked from the outside. He was also keenly aware of the two large beasts still closely behind him. They were prodded along until they reached the center, where an even larger beast awaited. Its reptilian skin did not vary in color like the others. It was completely gray, wonderfully patterned in diamond-like shapes. Crouched down on large, clawed feet, this 'Gray Bird' sat ominously in front of them, watching them with sharp, piercing eyes. Willem looked around, his mind racing, searching for any possible avenue of escape. Genella stayed close to him, taking in her surroundings with frightened glances.

The other two creatures took their place to the left and right of the Gray Bird, forming a semi-circle around the intruders. Gray Bird tilted its head from side to side as if trying to remove a kink in its long neck and fluttered one wing upon its breast. A rumbling, crackling hiss escaped from its throat. This was followed by another, different in tone and pitch. At last, a short scratchy sound escaped which sounded suspiciously close to 'a-hem'.

"What do you call yourselves?" Gray Bird said. Its voice, deep and crackling, surprised Willem in the language of his own tongue.

"M-my name is Willem and she is..." By the sacred moons, he could not even remember her name!

"I am Genella," she said.

Gray Bird rotated its head slowly, almost lazily before looking upon them again.

"You have not understood. What are you?"

Willem looked nervously at Genella and wrinkled his brow, puzzled.

"I don't -"

A quick progression of vocal squelching cackled from the creature on the left. Its skin a dark yellow and black, hung loosely on an outline of bones. Even the skin on its face drooped slightly, giving the impression of old age. The squawking, almost coughing sound it made before attempting to speak contributed to that impression.

"What manner of species are you?" The old squawker asked.

"We are Taymun." Willem stood up straight, beginning to feel a new found courage. "Saved by an unknown entity from our dying world and brought here over two hundred generations ago. Who are you?"

The beast on the right jerked its head sideways and a ripple flowed through its shiny black body. As it did this, hints of an elusive purplish tint streaked through its skin. It was when this one's eyes widened Willem noticed with no comfort its pupils were slit like that of a snake. Taking no time to adjust to their vocalization, this menacing-looking beast spoke quickly in a hissing manner.

"What is this entity you speak of?" It said.

"W-we do not know," Genella said. "Our people wait for its return so that we may repay the act of generosity that was given to us."

Gray Bird stretched again, revealing two small arms previously camouflaged in the grayness. At the end of these arms was a pair of small, childlike hands. It clasped them together, forming the impression of astute consideration.

"When is the entity to return?"

"We don't know," Willem said. "We don't even know if it will return. Some, like me, could care less and some pray to it like some sort of god. What I want to know is: Who and what are you?"

"This one is full of lies," Menacing Beast hissed. "And I can feel the hatred in its very soul. They must all be removed from our world."

"They are afraid," Old Squawker said. "We have no reason to doubt their statements."

Willem looked back at the entrance. Some of the Beasts were just outside, guarding against escape. Even if there was a way out, where would they go? Although he had not actually seen any of them in flight, he did not doubt that they could perform such a feat. Earlier experience dictated that they moved very quickly when they wanted to.

"Are you frightened of us?" Gray Bird said.

Willem wanted to scream at them. To get it through their thick, bird-like skulls that not only were they unafraid, they would go down fighting, if necessary. He was about to do just that when he heard a soft crying from Genella.

"Yes, we are very afraid. Please let us go. Let us go home."

"This is our home," Gray Bird explained. "We cannot let you stay."

"What do you mean 'your home'?" Willem demanded. "We've never seen your kind before. I don't know what this place is, but it looks nothing like our home. It doesn't even look like our world!"

Menacing Beast hissed loudly and took a quick step closer to them.

"This is not your world. You do not belong here."

"They do not understand," Old Squawker hissed back at Menacing Beast. Willem began to feel as if the old one might be their only ally. It turned back in the direction of Gray Bird with a slight extension of a frame-like wing. "They are of a linear existence. They must be made to understand."

Gray Bird again tilted his head before speaking. The quick tilt reached a full parallel with the ground and again there was a slight ruffling of wings.

"Time has but one direction for you," it said. "You begin at one point and follow only one line to reach your eventual destination. This is all you know. This is your nature. For us, time has many directions. We begin at one point and extend outward in all directions to reach our destinations."

"You think we are stupid," Willem retorted. "You think we don't understand what you are talking about? Our people have studied the possibility of non-linear existence. We understand many things. We don't live in primitive villages on barren wastelands like this. We are a civilized race."

"If you do understand our existence," Gray Bird said in a tone that could be construed as sardonic, "then you must also understand that your people have encroached upon us. You have trespassed on our world. And what you perceive as 'primitive' is merely our comfort. We require little more than this."

Genella's voice quivered when she spoke.

"How can we be in your way? We have lived in peace on our home for so long. Yet you say we are trespassing. Not one of our people has ever seen you."

"It is a difficult thing for a linear being to grasp," said Old Squawker. "Our race has expanded since our beginnings, branching out in different places and times. Your place and time of existence on our world is very minute. However, your existence will interfere with ours if we allow you to stay."

Willem voiced Genella's silent question.

"Why should we believe that you were here before us?"

"It mocks us," Menacing Beast said in a shrill tone. "Let me have this one."

Gray Bird thrust out a magnificent wing in Menacing Beast's direction, silencing the aggression at once. Menacing Beast moved quickly back and turned its head away.

"There is no point in attempting to prove our claim

to this world," Gray Bird said. "We were here indefinitely before and after you. We have brought the two of you here first so that we may be certain of your simple displacement. The entity you speak of is a possible concern, but will be dealt with in time as necessary. Soon, there will be others of your kind brought here. Your people must all be displaced."

"Displaced?" Genella asked, "What does that mean?"

"You will be...removed," Gray Bird explained, "to a time before your beginning on this world. You will become one with your ancestors. You will not be subject to the destruction that other races suffered in our many pasts. There will be no pain for your people. However, your ancestors must bear the burden of the displacement. In the era in which your people reach our world, we must this time refuse trespass. Perhaps the entity you speak of will find another place and time for them."

"Or maybe they'll die." Willem was furious. "You have no right to do this to us. If this is really your world, there are other things we can do. We could move to a different area, far away from where we are now."

"It is not possible," Old Squawker explained. "It is not so much as where you are as it is when you exist. We could displace you to many different places and times on our world. Yet, eventually, either in our future or past, you would be in trespass. It would only mean the bitter destruction of your people."

Gray Bird stretched upward to the full length of its being and spread ominous wings outward in both directions. Its head pushed upward and a shrill squawk beckoned to the beasts they originally encountered. The head turned again downward and spoke its last words in Willem's direction.

"They will take you to your destination."

Willem was guided along with Genella grudgingly to the exit. He turned to catch menacing expressions from their two initial captors. Near the opening, Willem moved closer to Genella.

"When we're in the open, run," he whispered. "We'll go in different directions and take our chances." Genella nodded her head quickly, but the fear in her expression told him she realized how small their chances were.

The bright sunlight hurt their unsuspecting eyes and the gray, rocky terrain glittered brightly in all directions. Unexpectedly, the two guards paused momentarily and seemed to be preparing for something. They ruffled their wings and stretched their necks in awkward positions as Willem and Genella continued on. This was the only chance.

"Run!" Willem told her, and they split off from each other, and headed for a separate rocky incline out of the valley. As he made his way to the bigger rocks, Willem thought they might actually make it. With a few quick glances behind, it was evident that the beasts weren't going to pursue them. In fact, they were still performing their strange bird-like movements, oblivious to their prisoner's escape.

Willem saw that Genella reached the foothills, but to no avail. He saw the large, winged terrors swooping down from above. Their claws preceded them, outstretched and ready to clutch onto a scrambling body. Upon nearing their prey, they hovered clumsily with giant wings flapping and stirring up a whirlwind of dust. The noise from the wings alone was deafening, but the screeching sound that came from the monsters as they tried to grab hold was horrifying. Once they caught hold, the claws were immensely strong and could not be pried apart.

Willem saw the ground leaving him. Before long, he felt the cool air of the higher altitude and saw Genella's limp form held firmly by the creature they were following. He tried to call out to her, hoping that she was still alive. His breath was quickly disappearing, however, as the mighty claws tightened around him. He saw bright little pin-pricks of light swim through the air just before everything went black.

The terrain was different here. Although the surface was still cluttered with an over-abundance of rocks, the rolling plain was gone. The flatness stretched outward, occasionally interrupted by groups of green trees and shrubbery, appearing to be tiny oases on an otherwise barren world. The air was cooler now. The sky had turned into a wondrous pink-orange as the sun made its decline to the horizon. Willem and Genella's still bodies lay in front of a large, almost rectangular stone structure. The abductors were not far away, stretching, picking and ruffling their wings in a bird-like fashion.

Willem slowly opened his eyes and fought to regain focus. The sky above appeared darker now, but yet peaceful. Perhaps there was a chance that this was all an awful dream. He rolled his head slightly and could see Genella's form sprawled out on the ground just a short distance from him. At first he was alarmed, but her face looked content and he could see that she was breathing. As he watched, her eyes fluttered open and for a brief instance she looked at him and appeared relieved, almost happy that he was there. Suddenly, the face of one of the creatures appeared next to her, its sharp, menacing eyes squinting down and its beak opened to reveal perfect rows of razor sharp teeth. A long, forked tongue slithered in and out quickly as if considering Genella for its next meal. The thing let out an ear-shattering squawk and rolled its head back. Genella screamed and scrambled next to Willem who instinctively pulled her next to him.

Willem jumped to his feet and lunged at the beast. He expected at least to catch it off guard, perhaps throw it off balance. He was stopped short when one of the small arms latched onto his shoulder. With one flex of its wing, Willem was thrown outward with great force and speed. His body slid easily across the gravel. The other beast stood still nearby with sinister eyes reflecting the sunset, seemingly unaware of what was taking place.

A dazed Willem shook his head. He was fighting mad now, but he had to find a new strategy. He looked around for something, anything he could use for a weapon. Genella ran to him and took hold of his arm with both hands, pleading.

"Don't do this, they'll kill you. They're too strong for us to fight."

He stopped long enough to let her words sink in, and then threw his arms up in exasperation.

"Then why don't they kill us? What are they waiting for?"

"I don't know," Genella said, "but I don't want to

give them a good reason." Her cold stare met his and Willem was surprised. Her carefree expression and laughing eyes were quite capable of changing into determination and seriousness. He wanted to kick himself for putting them both in danger.

The beast stood near its companion again, unconcerned with the last encounter. They surveyed the landscape closely, heads nearing the ground. For a moment, Willem thought they were going to peck at the ground for something to eat. After all he had seen, he once again found it hard to believe that they were of an intelligent species. His final observation told him that they appeared to be waiting for something. It might even be accurate to describe them as being bored with their current situation.

The air grew stronger and cooler, and the sky lost its gracious color to be replaced by a darkening purple. Willem considered the darkness. Could these beasts see in the dark? Perhaps this could be a means of escape, but where would they go? When the beasts had taken him into the air, he saw no signs of civilization for as far as could be seen. The whole situation seemed futile, but he was never one to stand by and have his fate chosen for him. Perhaps he could reason with them. But, he believed that these particular creatures were not versed in his language. It was possible they were lower forms of life compared to the ones that spoke. Perhaps they served the others as simple workers; having the gift of flight, but not so gifted in the cranial area.

He did not get the chance for attempted communication. They both looked up suddenly from their brooding, and one cocked its head with dog-like consistency. They approached Willem and Genella.

It was not a menacing advance, but more of an expectant one. They faced the large stone that lay just beyond their two prisoners. Willem followed their gaze onto the face of the stone. At once, the smooth surface wavered, and a large circle began to form. It was the blue and pink swirl of the vortex.

The creatures moved in on them and spread their massive wings outward, leaving the vortex as the only escape. Willem and Genella stood fast, holding tightly to one another.

"Where will this take us?" Willem said.

As if in response, the one on the right suddenly pushed its neck forward, screeching fiercely. Willem stepped backwards out of fright. He knew they were getting close to the vortex and he felt its strong pull. He tried frantically to regain ground, but it was too late. The creature's sinister face disappeared in a swirl of pink and blue as they were pulled in.

Willem came to rest quite easily on a soft and shiny surface. The vortex vanished, revealing six gray walls that looked identical. There was no orientation here. No up, down, left or right. He and Genella walked around the walls of their confine. The cube appeared impenetrable and completely silent. Willem realized there was no source of air, but he could speak. There was no apparent source of light, but he could see. Genella sat down and rested in a corner. Willem pounded his fist into the wall closest to him, sending waves of pain into his hand.

"This is my fault," Genella said. "I wanted to see what the serpent was." She paused in self-reflection and looked at him. "I've watched you so many times commanding the air around you and amazing those poor fools..."

He kicked the stone wall hard with his feet. There was no vibration, only a light tap when his foot struck the wall squarely. He backed up against the wall and ran to the opposite one, throwing the full force of his body against it, only succeeding in rendering more pain.

Genella seemed oblivious to his attempts. She continued with her absent-minded monologue.

"...they actually believed you were dead when you disappeared in the fog..."

Willem walked to where she sat and brought his face very close to hers.

"Listen to me," he said angrily. "I do not want to spend eternity in here. Are you going to help me or are you going to sit here and babble like a small child?"

She looked at him with complete honesty.

"Whatever our method of escape, I am sure it will not be arrived at by physical force. There are other ways of solving our dilemma."

"Well, I would very much like to hear about them. But you don't have any, do you? You would rather sit here and criticize my attempts than try to help. We have to find a way out of here."

"And go where?" Genella stood up. "If you could break these walls, what would be beyond them? A barren world where our home does not exist? Empty space?"

"I don't know. I only know that I have to do something."

He pressed the palms of his hands against a wall and sighed. Genella moved closer to him and touched his face, turning him towards her.

"We will do something. We will find a way, but

any answer we find will come from within ourselves."

Willem smiled bleakly at her.

"You seem so certain of that," he said.

"I know we will find a way together."

They drew closer and Willem could feel the remaining exasperation and fear draining from his body. He put his arms around her and held her tight. Perhaps she was right. Perhaps there was some way out of this. There had to be. He looked into her eyes and realized she had been crying. But there was courage and determination there as well and it filled him with admiration. He felt as if he was only beginning to see how special she was. There was something else in her eyes, too and it beckoned him closer to her. As they kissed, he felt his heart expand emotionally as if enveloped with enormous energy. He pulled back, astonished.

"What was that?"

"My talent is of a telekinetic nature," she explained, smiling. "I can use it to decrease your painful feelings and to enhance your positive ones."

"I don't need any help controlling my feelings," he said.

"I'm sorry, Willem, I just wanted to make you feel better."

He moved close to her again.

"I do feel better when I'm near you. And I'm glad that I'm not in this prison alone." He looked into her eyes and then around the confines of the cube. "Perhaps you can use your talent in a different way. Can you teach me?"

Willem sat facing his companion in the cube. His

hands were pressed together with hers, eyes closed, and locked in deep concentration. They were not alone anymore. Similar cubes appeared on all sides. Attaching to the original cube in amazing geometrical configurations, they multiplied and stretched outward as far as the eye could see. In each one was at least one person or more. All of the walls were completely transparent now, but it was impossible to communicate between cubes. The beasts were slowly trapping the entire Taymun race.

It was Genella who first hypothesized they must be in a place that is subject to the manipulation of time itself. Once captured, the entire race could be sent to whatever destination awaiting them. Willem and Genella had no intention of waiting to find out, however, and he concentrated with her, frantically searching for a way to alter reality. He had no idea how much time was spent in the attempt. All comprehension of time was uncertain within the cubes. But during one desperate effort, the space around them began to waver and fluctuate like tiny ripples in water.

Guided by a powerful entity of unknown origin, thirty massive star vessels continued away from their only home with no fuel and no certain destination. Yet they maintained a constant speed and direction. Adequate supplies for sustaining life aboard the crafts depleted years ago, but the race known as 'Taymun' lived on. They could not see the entity or prove it guided them, but they could find no other explanation. Something provided for them and led them on a set path.

Genella flew through one of the vessels, seeing abrupt visions of faces from long ago. She felt herself drawn to something and did not resist. The people she passed seemed so determined, joyous and full of pride. They had a purpose that drove them; they were looking for a new home.

At last her destination came into view. A woman of middle age let out a scream, in the process of labor. Genella felt herself become part of this woman, her ancestor. She also felt a soul-wrenching sensation of pain from the new life determined to be born. A great elation passed over her as the child arrived. When the baby was deposited into the mother's awaiting arms, she felt overwhelming love and joy as tears ran down her cheeks.

Willem was not having such a joyous occasion. Enclosed in the frame of an ancestor, he was fighting for his life in one of the darker areas upon a different vessel. Two large men held him in place while a third threw punches at him. He felt the air escape his lungs as he took a hit in the stomach. Pain coursed through his body, and then came a devastating blow to the head. They left him on a cold, hard floor gasping for air. A warm stream of blood ran slowly down his face and collected in a small pool. Willem could feel all of these things, and could also feel his ancestor losing his life. He had to do something.

Genella's soft hand lifted him easily. She did not appear to be in physical form, either. As she brought Willem upward, he felt a great weight fall from his being. The pain vanished and he looked down to see his ancestor still lying on the floor. He tried to speak, but could not form the words. They were apparent in his mind, however, and Genella heard them.

"We exist in a displacement of time," she answered. "We are here and we are not here. We exist, yet we do not."

"How is this possible?"

"Remember? Gray Bird said that we would 'become one with our ancestors.' The only way to do that is to exist side by side in two different time lines. Yet, we do not seem to be physical beings as we once were. I think our attempt to break free worked. We left sooner than we were supposed to. I believe they intended to place our entire race upon these vessels in full physical form, but in a different time so that we couldn't interfere with our ancestors."

"I was never good in the studies of science," Willem admitted.

"It doesn't matter. I think I know what we must do. Come with me." Genella pulled his arm, and they began to float quickly away.

"Wait. That man that we are leaving...I think he is part of my lineage. He is dying."

"Yes," Genella said solemnly, "he is your ancestor, but we cannot help him. Whatever has happened here must not be changed."

Willem watched the battered form as he drifted further away.

"I'm sorry," he whispered in his mind, fully understanding that Genella was right. If he changed the past, the future could be jeopardized. He may save a member of his family that died generations ago, but at the same time may cause many others to die in effect.

They flew easily through the hull and into the vastness of space. Willem felt the fear envelope his soul as they did so. No air, no protection from the vacuum and no direction to flee to. Those concerns quickly dissipated, however, as they flew freely into space. He looked upon her face. She was smiling. Having made the trip more than once in her search for Willem, she actually learned to enjoy this strange travel.

"Where are we going?" Willem asked, astounded and in awe of their flight.

"While I was traveling to each ship looking for you, I came out here many times. Each time, I was completely overcome with the feeling that I was not alone. Can you feel it?"

For the first time, Willem took complete inventory of all the sensations that he was feeling. "Yes, I can. What is here with us?"

"I think that perhaps it is the entity that guides us."

As they journeyed farther away from the montage of vessels, their speed increased, and the space around them changed. It was no longer dark, but filled with swirling colors. Images of their past swam quickly around them in a circle. They tumbled into the vortex of light that lay in the center. Willem saw his companion fly away from him. Her mouth was open in an unheard scream as the sound of a thousand voices surrounded and deafened them. He reached for her, and his arms stretched outward, twisted and distorted. Her body was becoming that way, too. She elongated, became wavy and quickly lost her form. Willem looked at himself and saw that he was also becoming deformed. His hands found hers, and he held on to her with all his strength as they passed through the vortex of light.

Suddenly, they were standing in a dim place. Dark caverns welcomed them at every turn. Everything had returned to normal for now. But where were they? They walked lightly through a tunnel, following the source of light appearing to be just ahead. The tunnel enlarged into a massive circular cavern lit by twelve torches high above the surface. Walking across the cavern, they were drawn to a curious darkness upon the surface. It was a precipice of the like they had never dreamed of. It extended downward into infinite darkness. Willem kicked a small rock over the edge and it disappeared into the black. They waited for the inevitable sound of it hitting the bottom, but there was silence.

Suddenly, they heard a loud rustling sound, followed by a small thud behind them. They turned quickly and stared in horror. Menacing Beast eyed them contemptuously.

"You parasitic beings learn quickly, but you have reached the end of your journey," it scorned in a sharp hiss.

Willem pulled Genella close to him and stared at the creature. How like the serpents back home it was, he thought. With a coloring so beautiful, it cultivated your trust. How could something so enchanting possibly be harmful? It enticed you into believing that you could touch it. Then it would destroy you for your distraction of its beauty.

"You wanted to kill us from the beginning," Genella cried. "Why?"

"I am filled with hatred of your kind," Menacing Beast said, "Your ugliness, your cowardice and your infestation of my world. Do you not realize why I convinced my people to banish you? I lived among you, watched your habits and learned of your ways, sent to determine a possible threat to us. What I discovered, however, is that your people were nearing the edge of your next step in evolution. You were going to become like us: A race that can exist in many time lines. That is the only reason you have escaped displacement. Somehow you have accepted this change more quickly than the others."

"So, it wasn't that we were merely in the way," Willem said through gritted teeth. "We would become a type of being that could exist in the same way you do, therefore existing in the same space. Your race would have to learn to live with us."

"Something I would not tolerate," it retorted spitefully. "I knew if I told the others of your ascension, some would welcome your change with openness and trust. Therefore, I convinced them that you were multiplying rapidly. That your deceptive and warring nature would only bring eventual harm to our race."

Genella suddenly gasped. She realized that this creature that stood before them was familiar to her. It was not its physical appearance or any tangible aspect that struck her. It was the simple hatred and condemnation she sensed from its presence, the same feelings which eluded her before she stepped into the vortex at the carnival. Menacing Beast looked at her with sharp wicked eyes as if it knew what she was thinking.

"Soon your entire race will be gone," it said in a low hiss.

The creature approached, forcing them backwards until they were standing on the very edge of the precipice. A giant wingspan surrounded them, denying any opportunity for escape and causing them to lose balance on the edge. They fell into the chasm, barely catching the edge with their hands. The beast moved closer to the edge and slammed its beak into the stone surface like a steel spike. Willem barely moved his hand in time. As the creature continued its attacks, he realized it really didn't matter if he was able to avoid them. Soon, his strength would be gone and they would fall to their deaths. A quick glance at Genella revealed that she was already struggling to hold on.

Suddenly, something flew into Menacing Beast and knocked him onto the cavern floor. A wicked cackle of squawking echoed throughout the chamber. Desperately, Willem scrambled up to the surface. As he helped Genella gain footing, his eyes widened in disbelief from the vision he was seeing. Their menace was on the cavern floor clawing and fighting for its life. Old Squawker had appeared from nowhere and ripped at the beast's flesh, attacking with raw instinct.

The two creatures screeched loudly as they tore into one another. Menacing Beast seemed to be losing, when suddenly it opened up its mouth to reveal a long set of razor sharp teeth. It tore into Old Squawker's neck, causing them both to go into a battling roll upon the surface. The two foes tumbled towards Willem and Genella, and they jumped out of the way just in time before the beasts went over the edge. A large set of claws clamped onto the ground, and Willem ran over to see the menace try to pull itself back up. Old Squawker was further down, still clawing into its enemy. Willem kicked hard at the claws, to no avail. Then, he reached down, clutched a solitary claw, and twisted it backwards with all his might. There was a loud shriek as both creatures fell into the abyss.

Silence.

Willem collapsed near the edge with Genella at his side. He stayed there for a while, trying to catch his breath. Then, far away at first, they heard the distinct sound of flapping wings. One of the creatures was rising up from the bottomless pit. Willem held onto his companion, too exhausted to run and nowhere to run to. It got louder and louder until at last he saw the flying beast emerge from the pit.

Old Squawker appeared from the darkness. Willem could see it was badly wounded with blood streaming down an injured neck. The winged creature made it to a group of large rocks and fell sharply against them.

Genella ran quickly to it, stopping short of its battered body, not knowing what to do. Willem came up quickly behind and started to pull her away. He realized, however, that the beast would never rise again. It was dying.

"There must be something we can do," Genella said.

Old Squawker lifted its head slightly, once sharp eyes growing dull, a once majestic wingspan mangled and torn.

"There is nothing you can do for me," it whispered, "my time has come to an end. Your people have been safely returned. In time, your race and ours will live among one another. It is important that what has happened here not be forgotten, less another with intentions of evil arises. One who is capable of swaying the thoughts of those who foolishly believe themselves to be wise."

"It will not be forgotten," Willem said.

Old Squawker rested its head against the rocks once more and allowed the last breaths of life to escape slowly away. In its final thoughts, the creature felt its memories and the sum of all of its being passing away, transcending to someplace else. Perhaps the next step in its own evolution.

Author's note: Where the idea for this story came from, I'm not sure, except that I think I came up with the title first. Then, the rest of the story started to materialize. One time I was in a writer's workshop and after reading this story to a group of fellow writers, it was time for criticism. One guy spoke up and said that he thought the story was 'too linear'. Having had my share of criticisms based on writing clichés such as 'show don't tell' (which I have always been guilty of), I asked him what he meant by that. He said, 'I don't know, it just seems too linear'. Well, he may have been right, that's really for a reader to decide. It just left me somewhat amused as the entire story deals with the concept of non-linear time...

Jenna's Needle

Jenna lay on a gurney, motionless at the end of the room. Beside the bed, the heart monitor emitted a high-pitched, steady signal. The screen was also steady, flat-lined. Dr. Paul Weston was only stopping by for test results. He was not prepared for the situation that greeted him, but he flew into action under a controlling instinct, the result of ten years at the emergency center. All at once, he was verifying the non-existent pulse. Checking her over for any obvious signs of the demise. Pushing an eyelid back to check for dilation. He ripped her blouse open and fumbled in the nearby instrument tray for scissors. Where were the damn things? He snatched up a scalpel and cut her bra loose, pushing the material to either side while flipping the switch on the defibrillator. It was an eternity and a day until the green light pulsed the go-ahead. He grabbed the pads and held them firmly. He wasn't sure whether he instinctively called 'clear' aloud or if it was just in his thoughts, but he placed the pads on her chest, ready to jolt her with 3,000 volts of electrical vitality.

The monitor hic-upped. He held onto the paddles, not sure what was happening. Then came a few peak fluctuations on the screen followed by an almost normal heart-rate. On the gurney, Jenna's body convulsed violently and she began coughing like someone coming up for air. Dr. Weston ditched the paddles and steadied her as the monitor confirmed a high, but life-sustaining pulse.

"I've got you," he soothed. "Easy now, easy."

He noticed her forehead was suddenly drenched with sweat and the rest of her body seemed aglow with heat. Her body calmed almost as quickly as it had erupted. Dr. Weston wiped her face with his hand, glancing nervously at the monitor, half expecting the flat-line to return. Jenna lay in peaceful unconsciousness for a full minute. Then her eyelids slowly rose, but only three-quarters of the way. She appeared completely drained of energy. "Paul..."

"No, don't talk. Just rest for a while."

"No, no, it's alright," she said groggily. "I'll be fine in a minute."

Then, to Dr. Weston's amazement, she groggily sat herself up on the gurney and fidgeted with closing her blouse like someone half-asleep.

"Paul," she said wearily, "we were married for three years and I never knew of this perversion? Taking advantage of a woman who's out cold?"

He ignored her attempt at humor. "Out cold? Jenna, you were *dead*. You flat-lined. What the hell is going on?"

Jenna sighed and pushed back her long, dark brown hair, wiping away perspiration in the process.

"Paul, I assure you that I'm okay." She waved away his rising protest. "I know, I know. We have to talk about this, but not here. We're both off tomorrow. I'll meet you at Grady's at nine. Remember that little table outside where we used to eat lunch? I'm very tired. I've got to go home and get some sleep."

She slid off the gurney, peeled off a number of sensors taped to her skin and started for the door.

Paul looked at her incredulously and started to protest. Jenna half turned to him, still walking. She put a finger to her lips, silencing him. He stood there in bewilderment as she walked out the door.

The sun shone brightly in the blue Sacramento sky. A cool breeze canceled out the heat and made for a beautiful day. Paul sat across from Jenna and watched her sip from a tall strawberry daiquiri. She looked up at him with those sinister green eyes he fell in love with so long ago. She was getting older. A few more wrinkles materialized when she smiled now. Paul realized, though, that her beauty was not diminishing. She seemed to be getting even more vibrant and amazing with age.

"Well," he said, "are you going to tell me what happened last night?"

Jenna let the straw slide back down into the glass and stared at him. "It's the simple things in life that we should learn to enjoy," she told him. "We could easily be gone tomorrow."

Paul felt a pang of irritation as impatience his swelled. "You were gone last night, but now you're here in front of me. Want to explain that?"

She sighed and watched a pair of roller-skaters

dash past them and down the side-street. She shook her head. "You won't understand this."

He ran his fingers along his dark, clean-cut beard. It was the same beard she used to run her fingers into. Same beard, different man somehow. He had lost her in a slow, diminishing way. It was something he could not understand, but gradually she had slipped away. He let her go, opting for the only proximity she would allow him: her friendship. "I usually don't understand when it comes to you," he replied.

"I'm going to tell you, Paul, but understand this: Whatever you say or do won't change my mind about what I'm doing. You can report me and they can take my license away, but I have no intentions of stopping."

"Is this about that birth control wonder-drug you were working on?"

She almost laughed. "No. I shelved that about a year ago, you know that. No, this is something...very big."

"Big? What's bigger than...?"

"I was dead for five minutes last night, Paul. I was dead, but my soul was alive. I floated above my body just like you hear about from those people claiming to have near-death experiences. I flew like lightning, drawn towards something...I don't know what. It was amaz..."

Paul held up his hands to stop her. "Jenna, what did you use?"

Jenna looked away momentarily before responding. "Meclitrizene."

"What? Are you insane? That stuff will kill you."

"Well, Paul, that's kind of the point," she said somberly. "But I've added an inhibitor. I've been working on it for a long time. I can take the Mec at lethal doses and the inhibitor brings me back."

He looked at her in total disbelief. "Jenna..."

"Listen, Paul, don't lecture me about the danger or morality of what I'm doing. It may sound crazy. I may be insane by some standards, but I am going forward with this research."

Her dead-seriousness was hauntingly familiar to him. For a split-second, he was back in the very moment she ended their marriage. This was the same type of finality he was up against. Blocked out by walls he could not penetrate and her fierce determination that made him not want to try. As much as it hurt, there was always a part of him that wanted her to succeed, even if leaving him was her goal. She was somehow gentle, though. In her determination, she found a way to convince him that it wasn't his fault. It wasn't anyone's fault. It was just something that happened. He never wanted to admit even to himself, but he could not stop himself from believing the impossible. He held onto a faint glimmer of hope she would someday come back to him.

He sighed heavily. "Jenna, what do you hope to accomplish with this? You're a brilliant bio-chemist. I'm not going to lecture you, I'm just going to ask you. If you want to dive into this type of research, why don't you do it through appropriate channels? You have enough pull at the University to put together..."

"Because I want to know for myself!" Her fists were clenched and a foreign anger flashed in her eyes. "Haven't you ever wondered what happens when you die? Is this it? Is this all there is? If you adopt the answers of science, then death is the end. If you lean towards spiritual beliefs, then the soul takes over where the physical body ends."

"Jenna," Paul said slowly, "this metaphysical argument has been going on for ages. Don't you think that perhaps it may just be possible that we're not supposed to know?"

"That's absurd and you know it," she retorted. "Everything that we have discovered through science wasn't supposed to be known. It's a basic fear of the unknown that scares people. I am tired of the argumentative beliefs, of the 'scientific facts' that are left to interpretation. I want to know the truth."

"Yes, and what if you kill yourself in the process? I mean really kill yourself. What if next time you try this, you don't come back?"

Jenna relaxed and allowed a gentle smile to form on her lips. "I'll know either way, won't I? Look, Paul, I've had these questions for as long as I can remember and when my mother died last year...well, I realized that I have to find the answers. Think about it. In the larger scheme of things, our life is a brief flash of light and all that we were, all that we hoped to be...is gone forever. If that's it, if that's all there is then I have to know. If there's something on the other side, I have to know that too. I can't sit by and live my life in uncertainty. I don't know whether I should embrace every minute and push myself to the limit because it's all I have or if I can afford to slow my pace until eternity sets in. There's got to be a definite, unquestionable truth about life and death and I'm going to find it." She paused self-consciously as a couple, hand-in-hand, breezed past them headed towards the cafe. "And...I'll need your help."

"What?"

"I need your help," she said, flatly. "I've developed the inhibitor as a time-release. It kicks in to bring me back, but I've reached a limit with it. Now the only way I can go any further is to have someone inject me with higher doses to help me endure longer trips."

Paul shook his head violently. "I can't believe what you're telling me. I can't believe what you're asking me to do."

She looked at him evenly. "I know exactly what I'm asking. It's risky for our careers, our reputations and perhaps our very souls, but I need your help."

"I won't let you go any further with this. I won't help you."

"Then I'll find someone who will. It may take me a while, but I will eventually find someone adventurous and bold enough to do what I ask." Sighing, she slowly stirred her drink with the straw. "I would rather it be you. I trust you and I need your expertise."

"God, Jenna, do you realize what you're asking?"

Her intent look of seriousness dissolved away and she smiled again. "You were adventurous once. Remember?"

Their eyes met. He knew what memories she was referring to. Not long after they began to see each other, a foreign spontaneity took hold of him. One day, without warning, he made arrangements for them to go skydiving. She had protested, but his excitement and insistence won her over. They jumped together, later using the experience as a metaphor for 'taking the plunge' into marriage because it happened so quickly.

She broke his reverie. "Remember when we used to walk along the St. John's Bridge? I still do that sometimes. I always stop halfway and look down at the water. I can't help but wonder what would happen if I jumped. How long would it take death to claim me? Where would I go? How far would I travel to reach my final destination and what unknown experiences would await me? I know it sounds morbid, but my curiosity has always outweighed my fears."

He looked at her now as if seeing her for the first time. He knew her well enough to realize this obsession would not leave her. She was indeed serious. Insanity may be her driving force, but it was tempered with the intelligence and reasoning of a genius. He did not want her to take this dangerous path of ludicrous research. But even more, he did not want some stranger to help her. He knew there was no talking her out of this. She was going to go to do it regardless of whether he agreed to help her or not. He sighed heavily, relinquishing all of his reservations and objections to oblivion's care.

"I can't possibly imagine," he began, "what is going on in your mind to make you want to do this..."

She looked at him with gentle compassion. "But you can't imagine me doing this with anyone else, can you?"

Paul stared briefly at the people coming and going along the nearby walk, some in pairs, some alone. When he turned back to face her, his eyes were weary and his expression was one of resolution. He simply said, "I cannot".

Jenna lay calmly on the table. "Ten cc's Meclitrizene."

"Yes, doctor, I know." Paul filled the needle's chamber, carefully measuring the amount. Then he rubbed a spot on Jenna's arm with a sterile pad.

"Why so glum, Paul?" she teased. "Isn't it every man's fantasy to kill his ex-wife?"

"I don't see how you can find humor in this, Jenna."

"You're about to kill me, Paul. I'm nervous and your bedside manner is as bad as ever."

"You never complained about my bedside manner when we were married," Paul said, expertly pushing the needle into her arm. The deadly substance filled her veins as he steadily watched the monitors.

Jenna smiled at him. "Whatever doesn't kill us makes us stronger. Right?"

She quickly began losing her bright personality to a groggy one. Her muscles were going limp and her face lost its composure. Her words came out slurred and labored as she said, "Jus' don't fuh-get da inhibita."

"Don't worry," Paul reassured her. "I'll bring you back."

Jenna flat lined.

Her body looked peaceful as she rose above it. Paul stood over her, checking for signs of life. She drifted away. The further away, it seemed, the faster she went.

Then there was peace.

Complete serenity washed over her in an unknown world where nothing but calm prevailed. She flew, enveloped in a feeling of peace and security she had never known. Angelic wings, unseen and majestic, seemed to guide her faster than light itself. She felt it, but there was nothing to compare the motion to. Every possible relational substance seemed to be in a tunnel surrounding her, just beyond comprehension.

Then there was light.

Small at first, it slowly grew larger and she felt herself drawn to it like a moth to flame. She was not aware of possessing any physical form, but felt as if she were facing the light as she sped toward it. She believed her squinting eyes to be relaxing, widening. Tears streamed down an incorporeal face.

My God, it's so beautiful.

She wanted to reach out to touch the light, but did not know how. Suddenly, she felt completely alone. The worst measure of solitude beyond her imagination gripped her in its clutches and proceeded to slowly rip her soul apart. She tried to cry out, but could not. All of her senses disintegrated. She could not hear the deafening truth piercing her soul. She could not feel the interweaving substances tearing into her existence. She could not see the light as it began breaking into sharp beams that stabbed past her at lightning speeds. No stimulus was delivered from even her highest of senses, but she perceived it all as one. And she knew that neither her physical body nor her soul would survive this journey.

Then there was silence.

All the previous despair of her complete isolation melted away as quickly as it had come. A mixture of pure happiness and electric joy filled her as she beheld the beautiful entity before her.

Momma...

Jen, my angel.

You're so beautiful, momma, I didn't...

You have to go back now, Jenna. You know it's not time yet.

Momma, I want to stay here with you. Please...

Jenna felt something jerk her away forcefully. She was being drawn backwards. The form in front of her began to fade.

No! Not yet, not now...

Paul nursed a choking and convulsing Jenna back to life. As soon as death was no longer an immediate threat, tears began pouring from her eyes. She screamed incomprehensible words and lashed out wildly with her arms. While attempting to stabilize her, Paul felt a team of fingernails slice across his face. He covered her with his upper body, pinning her down like a determined champion in some bizarre wrestling match.

His mouth was near her ear and he whispered desperately to her. "It's okay, Jenna. I've got you. You've got to calm down. Everything's going to be all right." He kept whispering the reassurances until he felt the muscles in her body began to surrender and soon her breathing returned to normal. Through it all, her heart-wrenching sobs sent out pangs of sadness. As he lay there over her, he wondered how he could ever agree to do this to her. He resolved this would never happen again.

Jenna awoke abruptly, her eyes wide with fright from some inconceivable nightmare that her mind refused to recall. She lay still for a moment, staring at the ceiling and forcing herself to full consciousness. Then she jerked her head around, taking in the surroundings. There was not much to see. It was a small room, completely bare except for the bed she was lying on. The light was dim, but she could see a door on the other side of the room. She sat up and stepped cautiously onto the floor. A sense of weakness enveloped her and she wondered how long she'd been out.

The door was locked. She pounded on it and called out, "Is anyone there? Help me. Let me out of here." There was no answer. She slammed her hands into the door one after another and felt panic seize hold of her. She felt trapped and alone and began yelling as loud as she could. Desperation consumed her as she tried to make contact with the outside world. Overcome with helplessness, a feeling unknown to her, she slid down the inside of the door and started to cry. Even as she sat there sobbing, she wondered why she felt so emotional. She pulled her knees up to her chest and rested her head on them.

I've got to get hold of myself, she thought. *Just calm down...take it easy, there's got to be an explanation.*

A sliding noise came from the door. Rays of light shone from a small rectangular opening. A voice crackled through an unseen speaker. "Doctor, please try to relax. You're safe. We're going to turn the lighting up slowly so your eyes can adjust. You have someone waiting to see you." The small opening snapped shut before Jenna got to her feet.

"Wait. Where am I? Please open the door."

As the light slowly became brighter, Jenna went

back to the bed and sat down. Several possibilities passed through her mind. Perhaps she had been injured after coming back. *Post-mortem mishap*, she thought, half-jokingly. Maybe Paul had taken her to some discreet clinic so as not to get the authorities involved. She refused to entertain any of the possibilities for long, however. Eventually, someone would come in to talk to her and she would get to the bottom of things.

There was a buzzing sound and a loud click. A rather large man in a white uniform held the door open. Paul walked in and the man closed the door behind him. A feeling of relief came over Jenna and she hopped off the bed.

"Paul, thank God. What's going on? Where am I?"

"Jen, how are you feeling? Why don't you sit back down and I'll explain."

"I don't want to sit down," she said. "I want to know what the hell is going on."

Paul sighed heavily.

"Jenna, why didn't you tell me what was in that concoction of yours."

"What are you talking about?"

"You know damn well what I'm talking about. The inhibitor that you invented, I had it analyzed. Three parts Phenerol. God, Jenna, Phenerol? Possible side effects: hallucination, dizziness and psychotic behavior."

"Did you research my other additives, Paul? Did you find the Tri-chloral compound that counteracts the side effects of Phenerol?"

"Yes, Jenna, I know about it. It might actually work, too, if it were used in a living, breathing body.

The problem comes when you let that stuff sit in a dormant blood stream. It's worthless. Think about it, Jenna. The heart's not pumping, there's no movement in the blood vessels. How is it supposed to counteract anything when it doesn't go anywhere?"

Jenna shook her head. "That can't be. There are only a few minutes before the inhibitor brings me back."

"It's enough to render it useless against the effects of Phenerol. You've been putting this poison into your system little by little and now it's catching up to you. See these scratches on my face? That's what you did when you came back. You would've destroyed the lab if I hadn't restrained you."

"You have no idea what I experienced on the other side, Paul. Our minds aren't properly equipped to handle what happened to me. I'll be better prepared next time."

Paul looked at her evenly.

"There isn't going to be a next time. Do you know what you really experienced? Let me tell you. When you went under, there was still residual electro-chemical activity in your brain. You probably thought you were rising above yourself just like you hear about in all those near-death stories. This is indicative of fading electro-chemical reactions."

"No, Paul, I went somewhere," she protested. "I went to the other side. I experienced things that I can't even describe...I was so close to finding the truth, but it wasn't long enough. I've got to go back."

Paul put his hands on her shoulders firmly. "Listen to me, Jen. Whatever you think happened only occurred in your mind in the scant seconds before you came back. You can't take a hallucinogenic drug and not expect to see things!"

She pushed him away. "What happened to me was not a hallucination. It was real."

Paul sighed and examined the confines of the room as if seeing it for the first time. He said, "They figure this stuff will be out of your system in about a month. I didn't want to have you committed, but this is something that's beyond my capabilities."

"Committed? What are you talking about?"

He turned to her. "Jen, I know you're going to hate me for a long time, but perhaps one day you'll thank me. This is a...safe place for you. You're in the Sacramento Stability Clinic. They have good people here. They'll take good care of you."

Jenna stumbled backward against the bed. A feeling of deep betrayal came over her and she could feel tears at the brink of boiling over. "You put me in a mental ward? How could you...?"

"It's a minimum security recovery clinic, not a mental ward. Please, Jen, it really is for the best."

"Get out of here," she yelled at him. "Get out of my sight."

The orderly moved quietly in the dim light as he prepared Jenna's bedtime shot. He paused momentarily, noticing how rested and peaceful she was tonight. "Well," he said quietly, "you probably don't need this, but it might help you later on." He pressed his fingers on her arm, looking for a suitable vein. Finding one, he moved the needle towards her arm.

In one lightning-fast move, Jenna came to life. She grabbed the needle and jammed it into the orderly's arm, causing the big man to yell in pain. Recovering from his surprise, he shot around the other side of the bed and caught her in mid-flight. "That was not a healthy idea, lady," he said, dragging her towards the door.

He never made it.

Jenna emerged from a nearby locker room dressed in a nursing uniform and walked quietly out of the Clinic.

"She what?" Paul could not believe what he was hearing over the phone. "No, it's not necessary to call the police. I think I know where I can find her." He got dressed quickly, wondering what Jenna's mental state might cause her to do.

When he entered the lab, it was empty but the light was on. He called out for her and was met with silence. A small piece of paper attached to the gurney beckoned his attention. He read the note. It was written in Jenna's handwriting:

Paul,
I should have known you would confiscate my medicine. It's okay. I think you were probably right. Perhaps we're not meant to know. Whatever is on the other side waiting for us is only meant for those who leave this world, not for the ones living in it..
I want you to know that I always loved you no matter what happened between us. Some things just aren't meant to be, I guess. I want you to patent the inhibitor. If anything, it can be used bring back patients who might otherwise be unrecoverable. That's one thing I can contribute to this life at least.
Love, Jenna

Paul stared blankly at the words until a realization hit him hard. He let the note fall to the floor and ran from the lab. In his car, he punched the gas and skidded out of the driveway. It was nearly midnight and he was thankful that the traffic was sparse. He accelerated to dangerous speeds, running red lights in the process. He had only one guess, one chance of finding her. He prayed his instincts were right.

The car skidded to a stop near the east side of St. John's Bridge. Paul hopped out and ran up the pedestrian walkway that paralleled bridge traffic. He ran into the darkness. It was a good quarter-mile to the apex of the bridge and he strained to see along the guide-wires as he ran. Half way up, his body gave painful reminders of how out of shape he was. His chest heaved and the muscles in his legs screamed out, but he ignored the pain. Then he saw some movement in the distance and stopped short. As much as he hoped he would find her, he had not actually believed he would.

Jenna stood on the cement railing, clinging to one of the large guide-wires. The wind pushed her hair back and caused ripples to pass through her clothing. She was staring out at the dark water.

"Jenna!"

She turned to the voice as Paul started up the walkway again.

"Go away, Paul," she pleaded.

There was pure anguish in her voice that made his heart drop. As he got closer to her, he could see tears streaming down her cheeks. "Jenna, don't do this. You're not going to prove anything this way."

"I'll prove it to myself. I'll know the truth."

"And what if there's nothing, Jenna? What if you die and that's the end of it?"

"Then I'll die," she screamed at him. "If this is all there is, then life isn't worth it."

"Jen, this may be all we have, but we've got to carry on. We can't go on worrying whether or not there's anything on the other side."

"You just don't understand, Paul. You never did. There's got to be something more."

"It's the drugs doing this to you, Jen. Please, for God's sake, give me your hand." He moved closer to her. She was startled by his movement and called out in protest.

Then she fell.

Paul rushed to her and saw that her hands still clung tightly to the end of the cable. Her body swayed over the edge of the railing. She looked down into the darkness and back up at him, her eyes wide with fright.

"Hold on, Jenna," Paul said, reaching for her. He pulled at her arms, trying to lift her up with impossible leverage. He could see her hands slipping. She looked up at him with terror in her eyes. It was the terror of someone about to lose their life to a death with no meaning.

"Paul..." she pleaded.

Bending over the railing, Paul stretched an arm out until he thought his muscles would snap. Twin cables pressed firmly into his shoulders, ending his reach just short of her arm. He contorted his upper body and he felt something give, maybe a dislocated shoulder or cables parting just enough. He did not care.

He grabbed her arm firmly and pulled with a

strength he did not know he possessed. Finally, she was able to help him, pulling herself through the cables and collapsing over the other side.

Exhausted and relieved, Paul held onto her as she cried. All of her pain, frustrations and fears flowed from her in a heart-wrenching agony of release. Her soul seemed to be dying in his arms, but he believed there would be a stronger one in its wake.

Whatever doesn't kill us, makes us stronger, he thought, absurdly.

"I thought I could find the answers," she said, finding her voice beyond the hurt. "I know there's something beyond...what we are. There has to be a place where we can go. I just needed to see it, to know that it's really there."

"I know," Paul said, holding her more tightly, "I know. There were so many times you never believed me. You always had to see things for yourself to believe it. It's just the scientist in you. But sometimes..."

She looked up at him as if seeing him for the first time in a very long time. This man that had been by her side every step of the way. This companion she pushed away, driven by a blind mission to prove the impossible. This man that she loved and who saved her life tonight. "Tell me," she said in a choked voice.

He could see a light shining in her eyes. It had been so long since she looked at him like that. He fought for the words as they got caught in his throat.

"Sometimes faith is all we have to go on."

D.V. Nobles

Author's note: I really have no recollection of why I decided to write 'Jenna's Needle', except that the possibility of a scientist going to extremes to learn the secret of life and death fascinated me. When I checked it over for inclusion in this book, I thought for sure that I would need to rewrite the Near Death Experience (NDE) scene where the main character sees her body below. After all, I now had first-hand experience, at least when it came to traveling outside the body, which I've written about in my non-fiction book, 'Journey into the Unknown'. It turned out, however, that my description in this story was spot-on, at least for the parts that I can relate to. As far as it being accurate for an actual NDE I cannot say, but hopefully I did a little research for that scene...

The Hole

I can't imagine anyone who will believe the following story. Nor do I blame them. It happened back when I was in my prime. I've tried to find some of the old guys that were around at the time, but I'm sure most of them have checked out. Even if I could find any of them, I imagine they would either deny it or explain it away with some bizarre logic.

Anyway, I was there. I know what happened, or at least, I know the events that took place. I can't explain the why of it all, but I'm getting old and I figured I should at least put it down in writing while I still can. Who knows, maybe it will be useful to someone later on if the same thing happens again.

It was 1943. The big steel plant was basically my home. I spent more time there than anywhere else and I figure the place you spend the most time, it's your home or might as well be. We made parts. Parts for tanks, parts for planes, parts for ships and sometimes even parts for trains. We were under contract with the Department of War. They would send us the plans for this or that and we would make it. We never made any complete machinery, but just parts made to their specification. There was no sense of completion and little sense of accomplishment. From time to time, we would have visitors come through the plant or even the occasional reporter. They would see the various pieces being made and say, 'what's this part of? A tank? A plane?' And we'd say, 'No, it's a part. That's all it is.'

I can remember July of that year for more than one reason. In the plant, the temperature was unbearable. More than once, I thought I had died and was being punished for some past wrong doings. I can remember the blazing, red-hot look of molten steel as it came out of the nearby foundry. My mind easily reminds me of the unbearable noise and even the unmistakable smell of the place. July was also the month the thing happened.

"Anderson! Get up here...now!" The man with big, drooping cheeks leaned out of his office window. He watched the workers below, seeing them as a maze of very large ants, only moving much slower. They all looked nearly the same from the height of his office, but he could recognize Anderson from any distance.

The tall, thin fellow looked up quickly from his work. His mouth was agape as it almost always was. His round eyes widened at the expression coming from the boss and his long, squared-off nose seem to point him in the direction he should be looking. He stopped what he was doing and his long, lanky legs carried him across the plant floor. He looked around nervously at the other workers as he walked, pausing only briefly before walking up the steel stairway.

The boss man's office resided on a steel platform high above the floor. From this vantage point, he could keep an eye on the workers and point out potential problems. At least, that was the idea. A small walkway adjoining the stairs protruded from his door and continued on to the other side where another room was also suspended by steel beams. This was known as the 'cage'. It was much larger than the office and was completely surrounded by a latticework of mesh wire, hence its nickname.

I followed Anderson up the stairs, feeling lucky that I was heading for the cage instead of where he was headed. I held a few drill bits in my hand. They were dull from my work and needed to exchange them for some sharpened ones. At the top of the stairs, I turned the sharp corner at the walkway, but Anderson kept going straight for the office.

I caught a short glimpse into the office before I completely turned, seeing the boss fuming as he continued to look down at the shop floor. I felt sorry for Anderson, but was glad it wasn't me going in there.

There was a pretty, young lady working inside the cage. It was her job to sharpen the bits and keep them filed away in the correct boxes. I stretched out a handful of them through a window opening.

"Here you are, Lil. Nice and dull, just ready to be sharpened up."

"Gee, thanks," Lil said. Then she smiled and went off to find me some replacements.

I turned to the sound of a ruckus coming from the office. The boss was fuming and wailing on poor

Anderson like an angry locomotive with an endless supply of steam. He was all red in the face and you could see the veins in his neck pulsing under his skin. I could hear him yelling, but with all the noise in the shop and the fact that his office was nicely insulated, I could only make out a few of the words. Something about safety goggles and hospital bills. I reckon Anderson was caught not wearing his safety glasses again.

Lil walked back up to the window and handed me six replacement bits. I had given her seven.

She said, "I don't have any quarter-inch ones. They're all out, but wait for a minute and I'll have the one you gave me sharpened up in a jiffy." Then she stuck her head out of the window a bit, looking in the direction of the office and shaking her head. "There's no need in that. He needs to learn to pipe down a bit."

In a moment, Lil was back with my drill bit and I turned to leave. At the same time, Anderson was coming out of the office. He paused after closing the door, looking down at his feet. He seemed to be resolving to do a better job from now on. Then, he quickly started across the walkway to return to work. Just then, I noticed something strange about the walkway. There was a hole. A big, gaping hole at the end of the walkway and Anderson was heading straight for it. I was about to yell for him to stop, but it happened too quickly.

"Whoa!" Anderson stopped just short of the hole, bending his legs and fluttering his arms in an odd attempt to maintain his balance. When he finally settled into a safe stance, I ran quickly over to the spot. That's what it was, a spot. A large, completely round circle about three feet in diameter was taking up almost the entire width of the walkway. It was at the beginning of the path that led to the boss's office. The hole itself was pitch black. I would have sworn that someone spilled a splash of black paint or tar on the walkway, but the steel mesh that made up the floor of the walkway was missing within the circle. And there was something else strange about it. It seemed to have some sort of depth. But if it was a hole, then we should have been able to see the shop floor below. All we saw was darkness.

"What do you make of this?" Anderson took off his cap and scratched his head.

"I don't know. Strange." I bent down to get a closer look and slowly moved an index finger in to touch it.

"Careful, Monty," Anderson warned. "It looks like something ate right through the steel."

I paused when he said that, and then continued. When my finger reached the point where it should have touched the floor or the blackness, there was nothing there. It was odd, though. I could feel my hand being drawn to it like a magnet to steel. I wanted to reach down deeper to find the bottom, but decided against it. I withdrew my hand.

"Hey, what's going on here? Don't you guys have work to--" the boss stopped short, gawking at the giant opening in front of Anderson. "What the sam hill is that?"

"I...I don't know, sir," Anderson replied. "I almost fell into it when I left your office."

"It's...it's some kind of *opening*," I offered, not really sure how to describe it. Now, a few of the workmen appeared to see what was going on and Lil left her cage to determine what all the fuss was about.

I rubbed my chin. "Someone get me a measuring rod. I want to find out where the bottom is."

One of the guys took off to carry out my request and I noticed the plant getting quieter as men shut down their machines, curious of the upstairs commotion.

One of the guys ran down to the floor and looked up at the walkway where the hole should be. "I don't believe this," he said, excitedly. "There's nothing there. It's just the bottom of the walkway. It can't be a hole."

As I stared into the darkness, one of the workmen shoved a six foot long measuring rod in front of me. I took hold of it and held it up vertically above the circle. Slowly, I began lowering it into the darkness. Now, the plant was completely quiet. I never heard it that way before and it was strange. It was like everyone got together to take a break. Somehow, I was now in charge of an investigation into something that was yet unknown. I wasn't sure I wanted to be the one doing it, but I proceeded.

I continued to lower the rod. One foot. A foot and a half. I could feel the rod begin to vibrate in my hands. Not a lot, just a sort of humming vibration. Two feet. I was aware of a pulling sensation that kept getting stronger the further I lowered it. Three feet. I increased my hold on the rod with both hands, proportional to the pulling into the hole. Out of the corner of my eye, I could see over the walkway to the man on the shop floor. He was rubbing his eyes, trying to see the rod emerging from the bottom. Somehow I knew that it wasn't.

Four feet. I was holding the rod straight out in front of me with both hands, now straining to hold onto it. I could feel muscles on each side of my back that I knew I never used. I was going to ask for help in holding on to it, but a couple of the guys closest to me latched on to the walkway rails with one hand and aided me with the other. Five feet. I looked down into the blackness. The first few inches of the measuring rod were gone. The rod didn't look like it was broken, but *submerged*.

The force pulling it down was overwhelming. I grunted in pain as I fought to keep my balance and felt strong hands on my shoulders to keep me from falling into it. Five feet and a few inches. We couldn't hold it any longer.

"Let it go on three," I commanded. "One...two...THREE!"

We all let go of the stick simultaneously and it was sucked down so quickly into the blackness, we barely saw it. I looked across to Anderson, who was still crouched down and examining the thing. The boss was peering past his shoulder and into the hole with a look of suspicion on his face. They were the only ones on their side of the walkway. I was thinking we would need to find a ladder to get them across somehow. Then Anderson stuck his hand down into the hole.

"There's got to be a bottom," he said. "It just doesn't make sense." He reached down with the full length of his arm.

"Anderson, don't!"

I was too late in my warning. He wasn't prepared for the pulling force. Like a child near a hot plate, I thought, stupidly. They don't really believe it's hot until they get burned. He tumbled into the hole head first. We heard a slight gasp and he was gone.

Silence.

"Good God almighty," the boss finally said.

Lil pushed her way up to the hole. "What happened to him? Where did he go?"

I looked up at her. I didn't know what to say. I just shook my head. I heard one of the guys behind me. "Well, we've got to do something. We've got to find out what happened to him."

I stood up and turned around. My words came out more angrily than I expected them to. "What can we do? Do you have any suggestions? Because, if you do, we'd all like to hear them."

I turned to the rail, looking over the edge at a workman below. I didn't have to ask, he could read the expression on my face. He slowly shook his head. There was simply nothing there to see. I slammed my fist down on the rail, feeling the vibration of the steel tubing run down its length and looked back at the hole. An insane idea entered my mind. "I can go after him..."

Charlie, a good friend of mine, appeared at my side.

"Are you out of your mind, Monty? We don't know where that...that thing goes. If you try to --"

My mind was racing, trying to gather possibilities, trying to formulate a plan. "I could be lowered in with a cable. With some portable floodlights. We have to hurry. Anderson might be hurt..."

"And he might be dead," Charlie said, sternly. "We won't let you go in there."

I glanced around quickly at the faces behind me. I saw confusion as well as frightened and even horrified looks. But there was another emotion that I could see in all of their faces: determination. They were ready to back Charlie up. I was strangely relieved, but also with a great sense of helplessness. I sighed heavily, abandoning the search for possibilities and bent down to the large orifice. "Anderson!" I yelled. And again. And yet a third time. There was an uncomfortable silence around me and no response from my attempt. My voice was hoarse even though I yelled over the sound of loud machinery all day long and it never bothered me.

"He's gone, Monty," Charlie said, softly.

I held onto the rail beside me, gazing into the darkness. Somehow, Charlie's statement made it definite. I could sense the feelings around me. They were thinking of him in a kind of remembrance now. Just a few minutes ago, he was alive and right there. Now he was gone. I found myself remembering him, also. I didn't know him well, but you couldn't help but to like the fellow. He was one of those guys who just never quite caught on to things. The guy that doesn't quite get the punch line of a joke or who never seems to be thinking along the same lines as everyone else. But he never ceased to try, always there with a desire to accepted, to please. Almost like a faithful puppy, I thought. Maybe that's why a lot of the guys found it easy to joke about him or to play the silly pranks. He took it in stride and never returned those gestures no matter how much the guys teased him. I gazed into the hole, wishing I had got to know him better.

"Hey!" A voice echoed from one of the large roll-up doors at the end of the plant.

Everyone turned to the sound. I couldn't believe my eyes. It was Anderson. He was standing there holding the measuring rod. There were cries of triumph and disbelief as the crowd raced down the stairs. We all ran up, patting him on the back and slapping him on the shoulder as if to see if he was real. He was surprised and delighted with all the sudden attention. I made my way to him and gave him a friendly shake on the shoulders.

"We thought you were a goner, for sure. What in the world happened?"

The crowd quieted down and then Anderson spoke. "Well, I don't rightly know. I fell into the hole and the next thing I knew, I was out there by the paint booth feeling kind of dazed."

A voice in the distance took advantage of the space of quiet.

"Welcome back, Anderson," the boss called out. He was leaning over the rail. In our excitement, we forgot he was up there.

"Hold on. I'll get a ladder," someone in the crowd said.

"It's okay, boss," Anderson said. "Just jump into the hole. It doesn't hurt."

The boss looked nervously at the opening. "No thanks. I'll wait for the ladder."

"I'll do it." This was from Rex. He was a younger guy, always ready to take a dare or be the first to prove something. He ran up the stairway and paused before the circle. Then, before anyone could say anything, he jumped in holding his nose like he was jumping into a swimming pool. The hole sucked him in.

The entire crowd turned to the direction of the large opening at the other end of the shop. The paint booth was beyond it and to the left, out of view. As the seconds grew, the crowd began to murmur and in a few moments, Rex appeared at the opening.

"It's incredible!"

This prompted a few other guys to go up the stairs with the intention of jumping in. Two of them did. The third one couldn't force himself to jump into the blackness. We all started moving back up the stairs and momentarily, the man with the ladder appeared. He tried to prop it up against the walkway, but it was about an inch too short.

"I'm sorry, sir, this is the longest one I could find."

The two men returned from the paint booth and caused a few more to summon the courage to try the experience. I watched them disappear into the darkness and grimaced. It didn't seem like a bright thing to do, to me. I looked across at the boss.

"If you go back to the office door," I explained, "and get a running start. It's only three feet. You can jump across it."

He examined the distance, looked back at me and nodded his head. He walked back to his office door and seemed to be considering the ten feet or so that would give him a running start. Even though he was heavy, older and probably out of shape, I figured he should be able to do it. We backed up to give him room.

"Okay, boss, whenever you're ready."

He braced himself like an amateur runner getting ready for a school race. Then, he darted across the walkway. I was surprised and amused. I had never seen him move that fast before. I calculated that he would not only bridge the distance of the hole, but we would need to catch him to stop him. He jumped over the opening and the strangest thing happened. He was sucked down into the blackness as if he had gotten too close to a giant vacuum cleaner. Then, the opening *wavered*, fluctuated and seemed to suck its outer perimeter into itself. Suddenly, it too was gone. The walkway was solid and complete as it was before.

We all stood there in disbelief and then cluttered down the stairs, heading for the paint booth. The other guys that had gone into the hole earlier met the crowd halfway, wondering what was going on. We stopped short of the area where he should have appeared and waited. There was nothing. We began searching around the area and then around the plant. The boss was nowhere to be found.

The next few days were dismal and strange. Even though we tried to convince people of what happened, they would not believe us. Some said they believed, but talked in a kind of patronizing tone that was usually reserved for those who believed in ghosts. The work continued with a line supervisor temporarily in charge of things. At one point, the police came in and called us together for a meeting, or rather, an interrogation. Could they possibly think that every one of us devised this story in order to cover up a mass murder of our boss? No one would dare admit that there were times they all felt like knocking him off, but wasn't that normal?

On the fourth day, it was work as usual. A few of the guys started to deny that there ever was a hole. I argued with them a bit, but I knew the reason of their denial. There was a lot of ridicule towards us from the press as well as from friends. Some simply found it easier to deny what happened then to try to convince those that wouldn't believe. It was hard enough for those of us who witnessed it to believe it.

Towards the end of the day, I was running my drill press. I kept running the events over and over in my mind and wondered when, if ever, I would stop thinking about it. I was looking forward to going home. It was Saturday and the end of a long, six day work week. Lost in thought, I continued boring holes, but suddenly all the power was cut to the machinery. Many of us looked over to the main breaker box. Sometimes, during a storm, the main switch would go and have to be reset. It was a nice, sunny day outside, though. Amazingly, there beside the breaker box, with one hand on the breaker handle and one holding a cup of coffee was the boss.

"You guys miss me?" He said and took a sip.

Soon a crowd gathered around him not unlike the one Anderson had endured. The questions flew out, each different and each anxious for a response. He held up his hand to quiet them and finally the noise subsided.

"I don't know what happened," he explained, "I woke up four states away...in a garbage bin."

A small bit of laughter escaped from the crowd and then it grew. Pretty soon, the boss was laughing too. Later, he walked up, took me aside and said, "Monty, don't ever convince me to jump across anything ever again."

Author's Note: Very rarely do I write any period pieces, partly because of the dreaded research required and partly because I am more into 'futuristic' or 'alternative landscapes' types of science fiction. This story takes place during World War II, at a steel plant towards the end of the war. I'm quite sure I did absolutely zero research for it. Consequently, when I read it over recently, I noticed that I mentioned the 'Department of Defense', an organization that would not be formed until 1947 – 4 years from the date this story takes place. So, I changed that to its predecessor, the Department of War. Hopefully, there are not too many other embarrassing inaccuracies.

My mother makes an appearance in this story as the character, 'Lil'. She once told me how she worked in a plant and one of her duties was to sharpen drill bits. In fact, it may be the whole reason I wrote this story...

An Influence of Paradox

Upon hearing about the murder on one of the lower levels, Ben Gilland was not too surprised. Although things had been quiet for a while, he knew it was only a matter of time. Things were out of hand down there and he personally believed it would not be long before the violence progressed up through the world and into the mid and upper levels. It just seemed inevitable.

He arrived in lower level 'C' just as the excitement seemed to be dying down. Each time he visited the lower levels things looked progressively worse. Overcrowding, filth and disrespect for authority. Walking towards the cubical, a hundred eyes watched his every move through the narrow corridor.

A woman stuck her neck out of her cubical doorway and babbled, "He got what he deserved, that's what he did. It'll be one less in the way." Her face was dirty and her hair scraggly. She was missing a few front teeth while the rest were yellow and rotten.

Ben ignored her and noticed the corridor was thickening with occupants trying to get a glimpse of what was going on. He pushed and waded through them until finally, the victim's cubical came into view. When he placed his hand onto the access panel, the door clicked open. Jess, his assistant, was already there and bending over the corpse. She looked up when he came in.

"Ben. Over here," she said.

The small room seemed a bit crowded with only a couple of people in it. As Ben got closer, he noticed the blood.

"Cause of death?" He asked Jess, even as he moved the victim's bloodstained shirt and revealed the answer. Multiple stab wounds to the mid-section.

"Somebody gutted him pretty good, Ben," Jess said dryly. "Of course, there's five hundred of 'em out there and they didn't see a thing."

"Okay," Ben stood up. "I need this room cleared. Tighten-up the security out there and get those people back to their cubes. Jess, did anybody touch anything?"

"No, of course not. We were waiting for you."

"Good. Give me a few minutes to comb this place. Meanwhile, I'd like you to attack those 'neighbors' out there, keep prodding them with questions. Somebody had to see something."

Ben stared up into the darkness from the bunk in his cubicle. As one of only two crime investigators in the world, his sleep was often compromised. His thoughts focused on the earlier events of the day. It could have been just another case of lower level dispute ending in domestic violence. He found no clues in the cubical, though, and Jess quietly pulled him to the side to make him privy to a bit of information. The victim was from maintenance personnel. Not just maintenance, but exterior maintenance.

"You mean like outside the world?" Ben had asked.

"Yeah, but that's not all. This is the fifth one this year. Seven months of similar killings and their all exterior maintenance personnel."

Ben kicked himself for not discovering the pattern. The victim's job descriptions came up on his file as 'maintenance' whether interior or exterior. As many residential murder cases as he investigated, there never seemed to be much need to check further into their occupation. Now some psychopath was killing exterior maintenance personnel.

He thought about what it would be like working outside the world, but could not imagine it. The 'world' as everyone now called it was actually their multi-generational ship. Two hundred and fifty-six years into their no-return voyage to the stars. Ben Gilland was 32. Thirty-Two Earth years. The ship approximated Earth time as much as possible for the sake of earlier passengers. Even night and day was simulated to Earth standards.

It was a very controversial thing for the home planet to do. Send a ship to the stars in search of another place to live, perhaps discover humans are not the only lifeforms. Eventually, with supporters out-weighing the opposition, the project progressed and tested the boundaries of world economy. The ship was actually three projects in one. When the designers discovered they would not be able to fund a small 'fleet' of ships as originally planned, they relied on a bit of creativity.

The ship contained the living, working crew. According to precise planning, they would inhabit the ship generation after generation until their destination was reached. Then there were the stagnant explorers; a crew of capable men and women held in suspended animation until destination. Finally, if all else failed, the most sophisticated (and expensive) robots designed by man stood by if it became necessary to act as a proxy for human exploration. The *Astronomous* carried them all at a small percentage of light speed towards their destination. The originators would never know of their success or failure.

When Ben was small, there were still a few observation decks open. He loved to gaze out at the star field, distorted though it was due to the speed the ship was traveling. He would imagine that he would be the first to spot their home world destination. It was a few years later when he learned he would long be forgotten before their arrival. Still, he had loved to hear the stories of Earth that his mother told him. The stories were on file, assisted with images of the past. There were certain details, though, handed down as far back as his great-grandparents. They were not recorded on file. It was these 'extra' things his mother added to the stories to make them seem even more incredible. Even now, he sometimes looked at the images and wondered what it would really be like to be on Earth or, for that matter, any planet.

Ben turned the events of the investigation over and over in his mind. Then, he decided to let it go. Answers always seemed to come easier if you didn't dwell on the questions. He was getting ready to dose off when suddenly and idea struck him. He made a bold decision on how he would proceed with this particular investigation as he closed his eyes again. He fought with the excitement and anticipation of his decision until at last he found sleep.

"You're going to do what?" Jess looked up from her work with astonishment mixed with concern.

"I'm going outside the world," Ben explained more slowly. "I want to know what they do out there. How they do it. As much about them as I can find out."

"Or maybe..." Jess looked at him squarely, "...maybe you just want to see what it looks like."

"I got images, I know what it looks like. Now, what did they come up with from the autopsy?"

"Autopsy? I didn't order one. I thought you were finished with him."

"I ordered it. It is possible that the stabs were strictly there to make it look like lower level violence."

"I'm sorry, Ben. That one's been incinerated. I don't know who you gave the order to, but they got it crossed somehow."

Ben threw his hands up in exasperation, shook his head and started for the door. "I'm heading for the upper level."

"Ben..." Jess wore a nervous smile and she hesitated before speaking again. "Let me know what it's like out there, will ya?"

He smiled back. "Sure." As the door slid shut behind him, she added quickly, "And be careful..."

Being careful was Ben's utmost intention even as he pulled on the exterior suit. All the while the instructor, a muscular exterior maintenance man, was jabbing last minute cautions at his new travel companion.

"I'll be right nearby," he ensured, "if you have any problems, just yell. The com works automatically."

"What about the weightlessness? What's going to keep me from falling?"

"Well, usually the sections we work in are structured to make use of the same G-force that gives us gravity on-board. The section I've been working lately, though, isn't like that. In any case, were always required to wear this harness..."

Ben felt a sharp slap around an ankle and noticed a cabled coupling now hooked indefinitely. Glen smiled and handed him a long roll of shielded cable of which one end was attached to the ankle coupling.

"Where do I lock the other end?" Ben asked, more nervous than he wanted to appear.

"You'll see. Now remember, there are hundreds of tiny handholds on the surface of the world. Just keep a hold of them, but even if you don't, you won't go too far. The cable will see to that, but you could damage your helmet if you hit something too hard. Okay?"

"I understand," Ben said.

They moved into an air lock and waited a moment for depressurization. Glen motioned for the end of the cable. He took Ben's and his own, clamping them loosely on a ring in the air lock.

"That's it? That's all that's going to hold us?"

He looked at Ben, his face appearing a bit thinner through the helmet. "I don't recall ever losing anyone yet."

The upper ring of the air lock opened slowly and Glen started up the ladder. His new trainee followed closely, not yet brave enough to look at the open space above.

Glen's voice crackled in Ben's helmet. "The ladder extends out of the hatch," he said. "When you get up here, just hold onto to it for a while and try to get a bit used to the view. I'll wait till you're ready."

Ben followed up the ladder, keeping his eyes on the suited figure ahead of him until he realized he was all the way out of the hatch and standing on the world. Slowly, he broke his fixed gaze on Glen's helmet and turned to look outward. He grasped the rung of the ladder hard. *My God*, he thought, *we're on the end of the world!* A few feet away, the edge offered a horrifying view of a bottomless void.

"No, wait. Look over this way first." Glen was laughing.

Ben quickly turned his head and tried to banish the vision. What he saw ahead made it a little easier. It was the entire length of the world. First there was a mile of relatively smooth, structured surface. Beyond that, an array field of some sort. Communication devices, he guessed. Then, the large land dome came into view. At first, he didn't know what it was. From the inside, you can see nothing but bright lights surrounding the perimeter of the dome. But from out here, Ben thought he could discern figures walking on the inside. He could definitely see the trees within. The distorted view of the star field he remembered as a child stretched around the dome and indeed, the entire world. Infinite points of light in every direction appeared elongated and each hinted a prism of colors within. Ben found it hard to comprehend the endless depth of space around him.

"Ready?"

"Huh? Oh, yes. I guess so."

"All right, now watch what I do. It's real easy, but mind what you're doing."

Ben watched as Glen squatted down and reached for a handhold. He was right. There were hundreds of handholds all over the surface nearby. He climbed horizontally along the surface using not only his hands, but bracing his boots up against the holds. The anklet cable unraveled freely behind him. Ben kneeled down slowly and followed, being very careful to find footing. They crawled this way along the surface for about five minutes during which time another view became apparent on either side. Long, linear pods stretched outward in either direction for what must have been miles. At the very end, the large reactors posed ominously against a star-streaked background. Ben's attention to safety was more or less causing him to store all the excitement inside. He felt like standing on the world and just staring for a while. He forced himself to concentrate on what he was doing, though, and listened as Glen's voice came over the com.

"Yeah, my first time out I thought I'd had it. I thought I should have got into another line of work, given the opportunity. After a time, though, I got used to it and realized that I was one of few with the privilege of seeing the outside world. I like it out here now. You know...if the tanks lasted longer, I'd live out here. How you doing so far?"

Sweat rolled off Ben's forehead and he wished he could wipe it away. His air gauge read nearly full, but he felt like I wasn't getting enough oxygen.

"I'm okay," he gasped. "You said you'd live out here. But...there's nothing. There's nobody."

"Exactly."

Ben suddenly realized what he meant. He lived in the lower levels like most of the maintenance people. The overcrowding down there was horrible. Yet Ben's level had numerous vacant cubicles. It did not make sense, but the lower level people kept to themselves. Ben figured the reasons could be traced back to the council laws. Earth laws governed the world, when it was started. As the years went by, however, the council continued to amend the laws supposedly to fit the needs of the world. It was agreed in the very beginning it would be necessary for the world to come up with their own unique laws, but the council seemed to have too much control. Eventually, occupational segregation went into effect and forever divided the world. Even now, although Glen was polite and friendly, there was a barrier present Ben could almost reach out and touch.

"Now, watch your hold. When we go down this side, we will quickly lose the little bit of gravity we have."

As he followed Glen down the side of a large exterior panel, it began to feel as if they were climbing down. The only up and down reference he had was the world, but the rapidly diminishing gravity was wreaking havoc with his senses. Ben had never been in zero gravity before and wasn't prepared. The next time he moved his foot to find a hold, he slipped and both legs floated upward. In a moment of panic, Ben fumbled for the right hand hold that would stabilize the flipping motion. His gloved hand missed and suddenly he was floating just out of reach of the holds. Glen heard his gasp and turned quickly to see what was happening. As he wriggled violently, Ben moved further away from the surface.

"Calm down! Don't panic." Glen was scrambling back to where the cable was within reaching distance.

Ben could feel his stomach tighten and closed his eyes to try to stop the sudden dizziness. It didn't work. He was getting sick. Finally, he felt a gentle tug at his anklet and floated down towards Glen.

"Didn't you remember what I told you? If you come off the surface, stay calm and avoid hitting anything with your helmet."

Ben floated softly down to the surface and finally got a firm grip on the handholds. They were now on hands and knees facing each other.

"I'm sorry," Ben said between labored breaths. "I guess I kind of lost it."

"You want to go back now?"

Ben swallowed hard. "No. No, I'll just stay right here while you do what you have to do. I'll be okay. I'm not moving for a while."

A sly smile appeared from inside Glen's shielded helmet. "Don't worry, you're not the first one to fall off the world." He crawled a bit closer as if it would make the communication more secretive. "Just between you and me, sometimes I do it for fun." He crawled away, leaving Ben with an incredulous, fatigued look on his face.

Ben watched him for about an hour, during which time he found a large protrusion from the surface to cling to. His breathing eventually turned into quick gasps and he could feel a cold sweat all over his body inside the environment-regulated suit. Quick glances at the air gauge became an increasing habit and a build-up of unsubstantiated panic began to siege him.

It's alright, he told himself, *it's just that I've never done this before. I'm sure that fall didn't help...*

It was to Ben's great relief when his guide came floating back towards him. He took another quick read of the gauge. About half full. He knew logically that it should be more than enough for the trip back inside, but it did nothing to ease his anxiety.

The maintenance guy had no clue why his temporary companion obtained the authorization to come out on the surface. As they talked, Glen explained to Ben that his job was to do routine checks on systems only accessible from the surface. He began training for the career when he was very young, just like everyone else. Nothing was ever broke, he explained, but hundreds of panels were lifted and checked by him and a few others every day. Just in case. The job originated fifty years into the voyage when some of the automated systems were damaged beyond repair. When the exterior components could not be monitored from the inside, it became necessary to do it from the outside.

On the way back, Ben kept studying the view beyond the land dome. There seemed to be something there, but the brilliance of the stars made it hard to determine. He finally asked Glen, "That area of darkness beyond the dome. What is that?"

He stopped a moment and looked ahead. "That's the beryllium shield. Traveling twelve percent the speed of light, even space dust gets compressed. It prevents otherwise harmless debris from ripping the world apart."

Ben was glad to step out of the suit, although quite embarrassed to reveal his sweat-soaked shirt. The maintenance man appeared as calm as he had been before they left.

Glen seemed to notice Ben's pale expression. "You gonna be coming out often?" He jerked a thumb back towards the air lock.

"No, this was a one-time adventure. One I'll never forget."

Ben shook Glen's hand and thanked him. The man was quite intelligent, Ben thought. He knew a lot about the outside and how the world worked. Sometimes it was unfortunate that people were born into their jobs and council regulations kept anyone from changing their pre-arranged occupation. He thought there were probably countless other occupations Glen might excel at.

Jess was waiting in the lab when her partner walked in. She reached across the table and picked up a mug. "Here, I've been keeping it warm for you."

Ben sat down and took a sip. "You ever wonder what real coffee tastes like, Jess?"

"This is real coffee as far as we're concerned. The old-timers argue that it doesn't taste real, but they've never tasted Earth coffee, either. Anyway, who cares about the taste of coffee? Are you gonna tell me what it was like out there or not?"

He rested the cup on the table and paused just long enough for Jess to raise an expectant eyebrow. When he finally spoke, his words came out with a boyish excitement. "It was incredible, Jess. Like nothing I've ever seen. Even the images don't come close. There's so much room, so much openness. I've never imagined anything like it, even in dreams."

"That incredible, huh?" She didn't sound impressed. "Well, it's not for me. You won't catch me out there. Zero-gravity, emptiness, no air...even if I lived long enough to reach our destination world, I'd stay here on board."

"You can't be serious," Ben said. "Aren't you even curious?"

Her eyes revealed her sincerity. She said, "The world is my home. Always has been, always will be. I just wish…"

"What?"

"Oh, nothing really. I just wish I wasn't stuck in this dead-end job."

Ben stared at her for a moment. He was beginning to realize he didn't know her as well as he thought. He said, "I don't understand. You've told me that you enjoy the challenge, enjoy solving mysteries."

She stared blankly into her coffee. "I used to. That was a long time ago. I thought there was a purpose back then, that I could make a difference."

"But you can…you *do* make a difference, Jess."

"No, not really. We are always there after the fact. We are just the clean-up crew. I'm sick of it."

"I didn't know you felt that way," Ben said. Her somber mood about the work was contagious and depressing. He decided to try to steer the conversation in a different direction. "What kind of profession would you rather be in?"

"What does it matter? We aren't allowed to follow a different path anyway."

"I know, but what if you could? What would you do?"

She glanced quickly away and took a sip of her coffee.

"It's silly," she said.

"Tell me."

"I'd like to…get into medical. I'd like to keep people from dying instead of dealing with people that are already dead, you know? I mean, don't get me wrong. I know what we do is important. I just think I could make a real difference if I had the chance."

Ben's thoughts drifted back to Glen, the exterior maintenance man. He wondered if he had any secret desires of working in some other capacity.

"Well, you know," he said, "they determine our major aptitudes when we are born in order to place us in the position most suitable for us. They can tell –"

"Oh, don't feed me that DNA determinational BS! I expect to hear that sort of thing from the council, but not from you."

With that, Jess left to continue her work in the other room.

Later, Ben asked his computer to give him an evaluation. He did not like what happened to him on the surface. Never before was he so engulfed with feelings of fear and panic. He spoke to the terminal, spilling all of the pertinent details of the experience and in return was bombarded by an artillery of questions. Within fifteen minutes, he had his diagnosis.

"Agoraphobia?" Jess was incredulous.

"Yes," Ben explained, "it's a fear of the outside world."

"I know what it is. It's just hard for me to...wait a minute. There was something about that in voyage research." She was at her screen in seconds and began punching up research topics. Shortly, a document flashed up. "Here it is." She scanned the contents.

Ben asked, "You mean this has happened before?"

"No, I don't think so," Jess explained. "But this research revealed a frightening possibility. That's why I remember it. According to this study, it is possible that a 'person remaining within limited confines for extreme periods of time may not adapt or adjust to a large spatial environment'."

"Meaning that I wouldn't make a good exterior maintenance man," Ben said.

"No, Ben. It means that exposure to any environment larger than our world would cause agoraphobic effects. You couldn't even live on a planet unless you confined yourself to an enclosed area."

"You've got to be kidding." Ben seemed to be more intrigued than alarmed.

She turned back to the document and continued reading. "The reason they never pursued this as a serious problem was that it was agreed upon by experts that 'occasional semi-exposure to larger environments would negate the ill-effects of the confined, limited environment'."

"English, please," Ben said, wearily.

"Well, things like the observation decks," she said. "They help to expose people to the larger outside environment. The idea is that as long as people aren't completely closed in, they can more readily adjust to larger environments."

"The observation decks were closed decades ago," Ben said. "Even the assembly chamber, the largest area in the world, was made off-limits because of the minimal radiation exposure. There's nowhere for anyone to experience anything bigger than what we have right here. You're saying that even if we reach the destination world, our descendants might not be able to go outside?"

"It would seem so. Long before the destination point, people are going to have to be slowly conditioned to larger environments. I'll get with some friends on the research council on this. I think you've stumbled upon a potential mission hazard here, Ben."

He winced. "Glad I could help, I guess."

Ben saw the walls in his cubical closing in, making him nauseated. He wanted to leave, to get out. He forced himself to relax and in the early morning, sleep finally came after hours of tossing and turning. It was then that a loud, shrill tone erupted from the bedside com speaker. He awoke suddenly, angered by the untimely disturbance.

"What is it?" He groaned into the speaker

"Ben...sorry, but I'm afraid we've got another one down here." Jess paused. "Lower level, section DD-A. You'll see the security."

"I'm on my way."

Once again, Ben walked quickly down a lower level corridor. Only this time, security was prevalent everywhere. People were yelling back and forth, mostly at the authorities, blaming them for lack of safety in the lower levels, living conditions, and anything else they could think of. It was just short of a riot and a few occupants jumped out in front of Ben, yelling profanities and complaints. Security pushed them back until he finally reached the cubical. Jess was standing in the doorway.

"Same method. Multiple stabs," she said in a fatigued voice. "I cleared the room, he's on the bunk where they found him."

Ben entered and clicked the cubical door shut, affording some silence. The victim lay in his bunk, face down. As he moved closer, the muscular form brought on a sudden, fearful suspicion. He carefully turned the body over only to confirm his fears. It was Glen.

"Dammit all..."

Jess was examining the cubical, searching for any possibility of evidence. She looked over to him. "What is it, Ben?"

"This is the first time I've ever actually known one of the victims. I mean, I didn't really know him, but..." Ben sat on the end of the bunk and rubbed his eyes. When he opened them again, the room tilted and swayed. He looked up, surprised. The walls seemed to close in on him.

"Ben, you okay?" Jess's hand was suddenly on his shoulder.

"No, I don't think so. Can you finish up here?"

"Sure."

Walking back down the corridor, hordes of people surrounded him on all sides, pushing, tugging and yelling. He waded through them, sometimes pushing harder than was necessary. There were too many people, he thought. Too many to be in one place. He felt a cold sweat breaking out all over his body and by the time he reached a more thinly populated area, his pace had become a dead run.

    The turquoise liquid was comfortable and massaging. Containing this substance was an isolation tank that was large enough to hold three people. Ben's naked form lay horizontally in the center with only a solitary tube running down to a small air pocket under his nose. He almost laughed, remembering what Jess had said about another frigging computer diagnosis. She was very adamant about him getting a true psychological run-down.

    An attendant studied a nearby projection displaying colorful graphs representing Ben's thought patterns. Every time the attendant asked a question, a different set of waves swept across. The turquoise gunk, along with its massaging benefit, also served as the wave carrier and provided the needed sensory deprivation for this type of diagnosis procedure. The very latest in mind shrinking, Ben thought.

    When the questions finally died down, Ben considered other things. Images began to slowly form in his mind. The exterior maintenance personnel. He could remember the faces clearly. The observation decks of his youth, closed one by one. Data gathered on the ever-changing space around their ship...eventually denied. The ship was getting smaller, closed-in. The outside was becoming closed off. With no exterior maintenance, there would be no one to go outside. There would be no outside. No, that wasn't right. Even though one must be born into a job, if all the exterior maintenance were gone, then they would have to get others to perform the task. Unless...

Ben clawed his way out of the gunk and pulled himself over the transparent edge of the tank, covered with globs of turquoise gel. The attendant protested even as he grabbed a towel and wiped himself down. "Just send me the results, will you? I've got to go."

Once in his cube, Ben tried to ignore the impending smothering of the walls and punched the terminal access keys. He retraced Jess's path for the information on agoraphobic research and correlated it with any possible entries on mission protocol; was there a reason to provoke a morbid fear of the outside in the crew in order for the mission to succeed? The answer came back:

MISSION PARAMETERS: SUBSECTION 17859.8
COUNCIL AMENDMENTS TO MISSION
PROTOCOL.
DOCUMENTS LOCATED: 0008

*** ACCESS UNAUTHORIZED AND DENIED ***
*** PLEASE CHOOSE ANOTHER TOPIC ***

"I hit the nail on the head," Ben said to himself. "I just can't see the nail."

He was about to leave when a soft tone pulsed from the computer. The psychological verdict was in and they wanted him to come in immediately and discuss it with them in person. "Yeah, that's not gonna happen," he muttered as he detached a small, hand computer from its mother and tucked it in his shirt pocket.

It took a good fifteen minutes with an acetylene-assisted laser torch to cut a manhole in the darkness.

In that time, Ben felt somewhat at ease with his surroundings while concentrating on the stabbing beam. When he finally lifted the crudely shaped circle of metal from the floor, the room below almost immediately began to sway. Even so, he stuck his head in and observed the surroundings.

The room was extremely large with transparent tubes running in all directions. Extending from every wall, long spikes of molded circuit cones grew like stalactites giving the room the appearance of some bizarre death chamber. There were also a large number of dark holes within the walls, facilitating permanent storage. Around the visible spikes, thin, amber lines formed concentric circles, providing one giga-quad of storage per centimeter. This was the primary data storage component for all information aboard the *Astronomous*. It was also a secure area lying beyond Ben's current clearance level. He figured he could have gotten in through the access door, but didn't want to take the chance of getting caught trying. What his clearance did allow him to do was disable the basic security system that would be in effect once he entered the room.

He studied the long mast that traveled the length of the room. It had several masts branching out on either side. He closed his eyes for a few seconds, hoping to lessen the swaying, but it didn't work. Bringing himself down through the hole, he swung loosely above the mast, one of his legs barely missing a circuit cone. He reminded himself how extremely fragile this type of storage was and dropped straight down onto the mast.

Once there, he recalled the storage address of what he was looking for and began crawling forward on the mast. He marveled at the memory growth around him, amazed at the massive amount of information the room contained. In his youth, he took a strong interest in computers and memory storage theory. At one time, he had hoped to seek a variance in his future job field and work with computers. After discovering it was impossible to change an assigned field, his interest in computers became a hobby. A hobby that helped him to excel at his otherwise unsuitable position of crime investigations and one that he hoped would help him now.

As he moved along the mast, Ben wondered if he might be in over his head. He hoped not. After all, this was just an oversized storage version of that which he was familiar with. There was a level of fear in his mind, though, that he might get caught. What then? He looked ahead and suddenly the entire room seemed to spin around the mast. The spikes went past him like taunting daggers. He latched on to the mast tightly and closed his eyes, feeling the mast turning in circles now. A feeling of nausea crept up on him and he vomited through the crossbars in the mast, adding to the growth of a memory spike below.

When he finally looked again, the room tipped lazily back to its normal sway. Cautiously, he continued his journey, taking note of the memory addresses near each growth. He stopped at one of the dark holes. It was just big enough for a person to go inside. A metal access rod stabbed into its dark center. The address matched.

"Lovely," he muttered.

Ben shimmied along the rod and disappeared into the darkness. When he felt his head press up against a wall, he clicked on a light he held in his mouth. A large spike had been carefully divided at key points and attached all over the cylindrical wall. The darkness served to harden the spike and limited its growth to nearly null. Ben twisted around the rod and examined the lower addresses as the light passed over them.

Upon finding the address, he withdrew his hand terminal and pushed two probes into the clay-like surface of the storage. He moved his fingers over the keys without looking until the read-out flashed: LOADING. As the terminal sifted the information, Ben looked back down to the end of the hole at the circle of light. Suddenly, he saw imaginary flashes of the cylinder collapsing around him, suffocating him in a memory storage bank. He wanted get out of there fast. He began to shake all over. The terminal was still loading. *Why was it taking so long?*

"Dis dam well be're be worf it," he said, talking aloud through the light in his mouth.

With newfound data safely tucked away in his pocket, Ben quickly slid along the rod and back onto the mast. He stood up and trod the crossbars with arms out to balance the inevitable sway in his mind. Once at his opening, he jumped up, just grabbing the lip and hoisted himself to the surface of the next floor. He carefully replaced the cutout and rolled over on his back to examine the new contents of the terminal.

In a few minutes, with search parameters similar to the ones requested earlier on his home computer, the screen lit up with information. He quickly scanned through the entries. A particular topic caught his attention and he brought up the text:

COUNCIL AMENDMENTS: SUBSECTION 748872.5
RESOLUTION OF COLONIZATION UNSUITABILITY

IN KEEPING WITH RESEARCH TOPIC 244A, THIS FOLLOW UP PROVIDES DECISION UNDER COUNCIL AMENDMENT AUTHORITY. FOR FULL DOCUMENTATION OF THE DECISION PROCEEDINGS, SEE MINUTES 1025.
TO SUMMARIZE:
THE QUALITY OF LIVING ABOARD ASTRONOMOUS IS IN A CONSTANT STATE OF DECAY. AT THE PROJECTED TIME OF DESTINATION, IT IS THE BELIEF OF THIS COUNCIL THAT ALL OF THE LOWER AND MIDDLE CLASSES AS WELL AS A GREAT DEAL OF THE UPPER CLASSES OF THE POPULATION WILL BE UNSUITABLE TO COLONIZE A NEW WORLD. AMONG THE MAJOR REASONS FOR THIS DECISION ARE SOCIAL CONTAMINATION DUE TO INDEFINITE CONFINEMENT AND INSURMOUNTABLE DETERIORATION OF HABITATION CONDITIONS.
A PROCESS OF SELECTION WILL BE PERFORMED BY COUNCIL AUTHORITY IN ORDER TO DETERMINE SUITABLE OCCUPANTS AS DESTINATION IS APPROACHED.

Ben was startled when his emergency locator pulsed. He thought, *they must be looking for me.* He snapped the terminal shut and moved quickly back through the myriad of access tunnels he had taken to reach the storage area. The walls were closing in again. He wanted to get away and felt the insane desire to go outside the world again.
What is happening to me? He wondered.

As he ran, he thought about the document. What right did the council have to decide who could populate the destination world and who could not? They completely eliminated all lower and middle class personnel with the wave of one decision. No wonder they limited the information to only the highest clearance levels.

I'm sure the council members are all considered themselves suitable, he thought.

As he rounded the corner to the lab, Jess and two rather large medics greeted him. The medics were dressed in mostly white with blue patches indicating job designations Ben had never seen before. Jess looked up at him with concerned eyes.

"My God, Ben, I've been looking everywhere for you. When I couldn't find you, I decided to use your emergency locator."

"What's going on, Jess?" Ben, asked, looking suspiciously at the medics.

"They told me your diagnosis, Ben. I was afraid you -"

"They told *you*? That's private information."

"Yes, I know," explained Jess, "but it's of grave importance that we get you to stasis."

"Stasis? What are you talking about?" The medics moved toward him and grabbed both arms. "What the hell is going on, here?"

"I'm sorry, Ben." Jess watched as one of the medics pressed a tranquilizer in his arm. The world became gray at first with what looked like millions of tiny particles flying all around. Then it went black.

"Ben, can you hear me?"

"Jess?" His eyes fluttered open lazily. He was in a large room and apparently strapped down to a movable bed.

"Yes, Ben, it's me. I want you to listen to me, okay? You're going to have to go into suspended animation for a while. I don't know how long it will take, but -"

Ben rolled his head slowly in protest, still feeling the tranquilizer effects.

"No..."

"Ben, you have a condition that has never been encountered before. Remember after you went outside the world? You said you had agoraphobia? Well, you were right. But because of your sudden exposure to an infinite amount of space after living all of your life in the world's confined environment, the effects are reversed inside the world. You are suffering from extreme claustrophobia. You can't live in either environment."

Ben shook his head slowly in disbelief.

"That can't be possible. I need to..."

"Ben, they're gonna need time to put some research into your problem. If you stay awake, you'll go insane. That's why we need to get you into stasis."

He tried to look at his chest where his pocket was and realized he was fitted with the same tight fabric that stasis travelers wore. "The terminal, what did they do with it?"

"Don't worry, Ben, I have it."

"Jess, Listen. I found out some things...you have to get some help. They're closing up the ship, Jess. That's why all the maintenance killings. There'll be no contact with larger environments except a selected few...that's how they'll justify keeping people onboard..."

"I'm not sure what you're saying, Ben. I don't understand what you mean."

"It's in the terminal. You've got to stop them...let me...let me out, Jess."

"I can't right now, Ben. Trust me. As soon as I can, I'll get you out of there. And don't worry, I'll find out what's going on and we'll make it right. Just trust me, okay?" She bent down and kissed him lightly on the forehead before they wheeled him towards the cryogenic chamber.

The door to the council chambers slid open silently to reveal the council master walking slowly in the room, clad in traditional black robe. His hand glided lightly over the highly polished oak rail. The beautiful oak that made up the railing, the stands and the twelve-member council pulpit was the only real wood onboard. Even the large audience seating facility was made up of the same, though the seats had not been used for years. A long table sat before the pulpit. It was used in earlier times to bring rebuttals to pending decisions. The entire room mostly resembled an old-style court rather than a decisive council chamber. It was a bit of old Earth nostalgia.

The master turned towards her slowly as she walked up to the table. His face was coldly stern and his eyes held a contradiction of grave indifference. He watched her place the small terminal on the large table.

"Is that all he had?"

"That's all," Jess said. "He's in stasis now."

"Good. And you will make sure he stays there indefinitely?"

Jess looked down and nodded. "We had an agreement. I get to change my profession."

The master gave her a single nod and she quickly left the room.

Someone once told him a dream could take years in stasis, but Ben thought that could not be possible. The dream was moving along at what seemed a normal pace. He hadn't felt this good in years. The travel through space was brief, but full of color and a fantastic rainbow of images. Then the destination world came into view. He felt his body enter into the atmosphere, floating softly down. Down to where he could begin to see the great masses of land and great bodies of water. The brilliant blue and green awaited him. Slowly, he descended in the vertical position and saw mighty forests of green and the grayish-white of rocky hills. He could feel himself smile at this delight and floated ever closer towards the surface to an awaiting green field. With his arms outstretched, he could feel the early rays of sunlight warm his body and, barely touching, he could feel the cool moisture of the grass beneath his feet.

Author's note: Surprisingly, as much as I like the concept of futuristic space travel, I seem to write very little of it. I'm not too keen on writing murder mysteries either, so I'm not sure why that crept its way in here. And of course the concept of one person having two directly opposing mental conditions may be kind of silly, but who knows what strange conditions we may encounter from extremely long-term space travel? I definitely like the idea of a multi-generational ship headed for the stars. It brings about a multitude of story possibilities and questions like, 'What kind of society would they become?', 'Will they eventually come up with their own system of justice?' and 'Will they finally get over texting on cell phones?'. You know, things like that...

The Lizard's Stare

Ken-ra sat in the midst of the dense jungle, frozen. He had been there about an hour now, although to him it had seemed a day. He sat staring at his menace, the lizard, who had also not moved since Ken-ra wandered upon him for the first time. The two stared at each other, unmoving, barely breathing.

Ken-ra was on his training mission. Everyone on his home planet came here during their youth to endure survival testing. It was only part of the training, though. The mental tests which Ken-ra had not taken yet could be just as challenging. This planet they used for the training of their young men and women was quite dangerous. Not only did it contain a healthy amount of poisonous and fierce predators, the climate changes could prove hazardous at times. Ken-ra was told by his older brother, Bie-lun, about some of the dangers he would encounter. One in particular, the one they called the lizard, had been the least of his worries. That was until he stumbled upon one in the jungle. He had been walking cautiously through the thickness until he heard a noise nearby. He slowly squatted down and, panning his surroundings, focused in on a lizard sitting eye level on a fallen tree not more than four feet away. It had not made the noise Ken-ra heard, but was merely basking in what little sunlight there was shining through the thickness. As soon as he realized what it was, Ken-ra froze automatically. It was the only thing he could do. He wondered why the lizard did not already strike him.

The lizard was somewhat different from the ones at home. These were bigger, more deadly, and had row of spikes flowing down the length of its green body. Its large, yellow eyes protruded from the sides of its head and watched calmly. Had he not known better, Ken-ra would have believed the creature to be benevolent and would imagine him as a pet in a glass cage. This was not the case, though, and his muscles began to ache due to his sitting in one place for so long. As long as Ken-ra did not move, the lizard would not strike. At least, that was the idea the more experienced trainees handed down.

After the first fifteen minutes of staring the lizard face-to-face, Ken-ra's fear lessened and began turning toward irritation. Why did the lizard not move? How long was this going to go on? He decided that if he couldn't move his mouth to speak to it, then at least he would make mental gestures.

Come on, lizard, be on your way. I have no time for you, he thought.

The lizard did not move.

From distant places in the jungle, a variety of loud wailing sounds could be heard. There was no telling what creatures were making all the different noises, but Ken-ra had hoped that one of them would be the predator of lizards. Something to make the lizard crawl away and leave him alone. Luckily, his survival training did not have a time limit. The ones who passed through the different test areas and made it to the pick-up point would complete the test. The more unfortunate ones would never make it. For the past month, Ken-ra had been successful. He made a few mistakes, but had managed to survive them. Now stuck in the last area, he wondered how long he would survive. He was no longer very fearful of the lizard. As long as he remained still, he should be alright. As time went slowly by, his worries turned towards other predators in the jungle that might find him sitting helplessly still.

If the lizard was able, it did not blink. Ken-ra did not blink often, but when he did the lizard did not seem to care. Ken-ra wondered how the lizard saw him. When he sat still, did the lizard notice him at all? Did the lizard only attack at the sight of movement? He decided that the lizard was taunting him. Staring him down. Waiting for the second Ken-ra would be forced to move, either from the existence of a more terrifying menace or because he simply could sit still no longer.

I can wait as long as you can, Ken-ra thought, although he wondered if it was the truth.

Ken-ra had no timepiece. He would not need it during his training, but now he wondered just how long he had been sitting. His legs began to feel a little numb. He thought about the absurdity of glancing at his timepiece if he had brought it. The mere curiosity of how much time had passed might be the cause of his death. He imagined the lizard noticing his head move down and suddenly leaping toward his ankle where it would sink its poisonous teeth. The thought made Ken-ra shudder slightly and even though he felt he did not move outwardly, the lizard must have sensed something. In one quick motion, the lizard's head moved up slightly higher than before. In that brief instant, Ken-ra thought of rolling backwards and running. He knew the lizard was too quick, though, and would most likely get him before he finished his roll. The lizard remained still for the second as Ken-ra almost shivered with fearful anticipation. In a few moments, the lizard slowly returned its head to a decidedly less-alert position.

Well, either finish me off or leave me alone, one or the other. I grow tired of the waiting.

Ken-ra stared at the lizard, wishing he could look behind him or at least any other view than that of his menace. Some of the dangers in the jungle were silent ones. For a second, he imagined one of those dangerous things creeping up behind him without a sound. The thought was so vivid and scary, he at once banished it from his thoughts.

He began thinking of home. It had been at least a month since he was dropped on this treacherous planet, but it seemed so much longer than that. He wondered what his family was doing. His best friend, Jen-sa, injured his leg not more than a week before they were to go to survival together. Jen-sa would have to wait till the next season and Ken-ra wanted to wait until he could go with him. He could find no excuse for staying behind, though. He wanted to go through the training with Jen-sa because they had talked about it all the time. It was always assumed they would go together as other friends did. They did this only to make their friendship stronger, not to increase their chances; no matter how many people you grouped with, it did not increase your chance of survival. In fact, it was best to face many of the dangers alone. Ken-ra figured that Jen-sa would be ready to start his survival within a week.

Perhaps if you detain me long enough, he thought, *Jen-sa will come along and find both of us here, staring each other down.*

The thought of staring at the lizard for a full week made Ken-ra want to cringe. He pictured Jen-sa stomping through the jungle, unaware of Ken-ra's predicament. Then, if he happened to go that way, he would stumble upon Ken-ra and the lizard. Ken-ra would have no way of warning him. However, it would take Jen-sa much more than a week to reach the jungle after his drop-off. Ken-ra certainly did not intend to be there that long. The lizard would eventually need food or water or something other than the gentle rays of sunlight. Ken-ra thought about the sunlight, too. If he were in this predicament too long, he would be caught in the jungle at night. It meant a sure death.

The lizard's big, round, yellowish eyes peered at him. Ken-ra began to notice that they did not seem menacing at all, but appeared to have a certain curiosity behind them. The only visitors to the planet had been the survival trainees. Perhaps the lizard was indeed curious about the strange invaders of the planet.

That's ridiculous, Ken-ra, these killers are just that. Killers. They act on instinct and could care less about your existence.

Ken-ra thought about getting to his feet very slowly and then running for it, but again he vanquished the thought. He would sit this one out at least until it started to get dark. It would be pointless to lose his life over impatience. He had been through the desert area, barely made it through the swamplands, and had survived the big forest. He had come out of all that with only minimal wounds. The most recent were scratches that still burned on his face. This was from the Gory Tree Bird that caught him by surprise. The marks would heal in a few weeks, unlike the scar his older brother, Bie-lun, received across the chest. He had tangled with the desert Gloom Rat. Quite a bit larger than a rat back home, its bite was harmless but its slicing tail could be fatal.

If the cut had been any deeper...

Ken-ra thought about the welcome Bie-lun had received when he returned home as a survivor. Everyone was so proud and happy and a celebration was made. Ken-ra didn't care about any celebration that he might get, he would be glad just to get home, to be done with it. Then he thought about his little brother, Ran-fa, and a strange fear enveloped him. He thought of when Ran-fa would be taking his training in a few more years. How would he survive? He was very smart and would pass the mental tests easily, but survival was a different story.

Ken-ra would tease Ran-fa about his studies. It seemed to him that Ran-fa was always buried in studies and never went outdoors. He never seemed to do anything. He brought home the high marks from his tests, but what else had he learned? There was so much more to understand than what the studies taught. There was so much to be experienced. But when he was younger, Ran-fa had wanted to go. Ken-ra would go into the forest to trap the game for sport and Ran-fa had begged to go with him. Ken-ra's constant reply was, 'You are too young, and you will get in the way. Maybe when you are older...' After a time, Ran-fa stopped asking and took little interest in his older brother's activities.

There was no time, I couldn't drag him along. He knew nothing about trapping. How in the world will he survive out here? He won't survive a minute in this place.

With no choice but to stare at the unmoving lizard, Ken-ra thought again about his younger brother. He didn't want to admit it, even to himself, but Ran-fa had looked up to him, had even wanted to be like him. When Ken-ra was young, Bie-lun had taken him to the forests and showed him the secrets of the traps. But when it was his turn to teach his younger brother, Ken-ra had no time.

His thoughts were interrupted suddenly when he heard the sound of something moving through the jungle. It seemed to be to the left and behind him. It was not very loud, but he could tell it was moving closer. He had to force himself not to turn his head to find out what it was. He waited and listened, hoping whatever it was would pay no notice to his still presence.

The sounds were quiet, slow and careful like something closing in on unsuspecting prey. Ken-ra could only hope that it was not the case. Soon, he detected movement on the left with his peripheral vision. He strained his eyes left and tried hard to make out the figure about fifty feet away, but couldn't. He suspected that the lizard, with its eyes residing on either side of its head, had full view of the trespasser. The lizard, however, did not seem to care. Finally, Ken-ra could make out the form of a survival trainee. It was a female with a large backpack, oblivious to Ken-ra and the lizard. She seemed to have a knife in her hand, or some sort of weapon.

Over here. Come over here and kill this blasted lizard.

It was evident that the girl would continue on her path and never notice Ken-ra or his problem at all. He decided he had to get her attention somehow. Being careful not to be too loud, he cleared his throat and then made a short, high-pitched sound within his throat and without moving his mouth. The lizard did not move. He did it again, this time louder and longer. The figure slowly continued walking away from them. Suddenly, and without warning, a large Devil Monkey descended from the trees and grabbed her up. She screamed in terror. In alarm, Ken-ra waited for the lizard to run or move in some way.

It didn't. He felt for the trainee, but could do nothing as he listened to her fading screams echoing through the depths of the jungle. Even though he had witnessed the horrible deaths of other trainees, he still had to force himself not to shake or shiver like his mind told him to. He realized that the girl might have been saved by his small plea for help. The monkey had been known to attack only in specific places. Perhaps if he had been a bit louder. Now her life and Ken-ra's new-found hopes of being rescued from his predicament were both gone. He then realized the great frustration of not being able to show the emotion he was feeling.

It was about half an hour later when the first evidence of sundown was apparent. Occasional beams of light no longer shone through the thickness and the surrounding mass of bright-green foliage was beginning to turn dull green. The distant sounds of the jungle were changing somehow. It was getting quiet, but it was as if the sounds were encroaching upon him. Ken-ra felt as if all jungle menaces were slowly surrounding him. He knew he had to do something, but did not know what.

What is it that you want from me? You want to keep me here until every predator in this jungle will have the advantage of nightfall? You want to prove you can stare me down? Want to wait until I lose my wits and try to run from you?

The lizard was so still, Ken-ra had thought more than once that it was dead.

Perhaps that is just what you want me to think, Ken-ra mused. Then he put the answers to his questions in imaginary lizard thoughts.

Yes, yes...as long as I keep you here, my enemy will come by nightfall and kill you for food. This will prevent him from taking me for food. We have this arrangement, you see. I trap his dinner and he leaves me alone. I do this to many trainees that come along my way. I already know I can stare you down, but if you try to run then I will kill you for myself and leave your remains for my enemy.

Ken-ra almost trembled at the thought and tried to ignore the aches in his legs and the occasional itch on the back of his neck. He wondered if this had ever happened to anyone before. None of the survivors that had the misfortune of stumbling upon the lizard ever mentioned having to stare at it for hours. You're just supposed to freeze and the lizard will be on its way.

I will call you the jungle Stare Lizard. How do you like that name, huh?

The lizard remained and Ken-ra suddenly felt a sharp pain in his legs. It was his muscles reaching an end to their endurance.

I swear, Ran-fa, if I ever get back home, I will teach you everything I know to prepare you for this survival. Perhaps you can teach me how to pass the mental tests. I will even teach you of the trapping secrets, whether you want to learn them or not. You will make it through this. I promise you will make it through this...

Without warning, the jungle Stare Lizard slowly turned its head away from Ken-ra. With its long tail following suit, it sleekly walked down the length of the log, disappearing into the thickness.

Author's note: 'The Lizard's Stare' was one of my earliest stories where I started getting 'serious' and submitting to the pulp mags. This is one of the shortest I have written and also no doubt heavily influenced by Robert Heinlein's novel 'Tunnel in the Sky', where a group of students are dropped off on a distant planet to test their survival skills. The concept of putting kids in a 'do or die' situation is a fascinating one and no doubt should be incorporated into the schools of today...

Sacred Heart

Fragile.   One rather small bit of land mass surrounded entirely and completely by blue, hostile waters. To be fair, a medium sized continent, but from above it could not appear to be anything but small and alone. Immersed in the image of the lonely planet, Watcher Sela gazed deeply, almost solemnly. She allowed her mind a transgression into the larger scheme of things. Where did this small place fit in?

Watcher Kenor mentally summarized the data. The people would never reach out, for they were somehow stagnant.   Apparently at one time progressing normally in intelligence and technical evolution, they stopped short. It was this fact that intrigued Kenor. A few of the lower Watchers indicated the desire to move on, to reach the other places. It was Kenor's place to decide. He decided to stay...for a small time longer. So much yet went unanswered.

Sela pulsed. Her glowing, yellow-blue form moved gracefully away from the Watcher station. She appeared almost humanoid in shape when her softly probing tentacles of light were not at work. She moved to Kenor, hovering.

"There is a change among them," she pulsed, vibrantly filling the space with a deep hum. "In each, there is a change when young ends and old begins. Self-inflicted, not occurring naturally. I am watching."

Kenor, a fiery contortion of yellow-orange, pulsed approval.

Delicate. Young Ren was on hands and knees with his face as close to the surface as he could get without touching it. One eye squinted and one eye focused on the small, round object several steps away. Another round object was very close by. If his aim was wrong, he would hit the other one, thus putting his companion out of the game. He had to concentrate.

"You will not get it from there," one of the players said.

"You can do it, Ren. You have to." This was from Ren's team companion, Cal.

Just the right aiming, just the right flick. He decided to take his time.

"Come on, it's almost ending." One of the many small spectators hunched over with hands on knees, urging Ren.

Met watched from the entrance, sitting cross-legged on the marble steps. In her view, the entire group of small children could be seen and heard. She did not see or hear them, however, as her mind wandered elsewhere. It began with thoughts actually focused on what she saw, wondering why the small ones do what they do. Why the strange, little games? Why the pestering questions and need to be of nuisance? Focusing on her little brother, Ren, she smiled momentarily. He was actually enjoying the game. Females were so different. They seemed to make sense in the things they did.

The studies were getting much harder, Met thought. It used to be so easy, but now there was so much more to think about, to wonder about. *Maybe*, she pondered, *it was harder because she knew it would soon be over.* The studies would be unnecessary. Met had to wonder what it would be like.

Suddenly a noise broke her soft gaze and the daydream was gone. She could not even remember what she had been thinking about.

"You hit mine! I told you..." Cal was shaking an angry fist at his team partner.

"If you hadn't placed it there, it wouldn't be in my way." Ren was up on his knees, protesting the outrage. Cal let out a growl of rage and lunged at his friend. In no time, they were rolling on the hard, shiny surface that was their playing area.

By the time Met reached down to pull the mass of two fighters apart, they were swinging wildly at each other, barely missing or scratching each other with inexperienced lashes. Their faces were bright red and Ren had tears welling up in his eyes.

Met dragged her small brother away while the fight continued its coarse with a verbal exchange of warnings, accusations, and foul intentions. Finally out of vocal range, Ren turned away from his opponent's direction and walked in exasperated silence. He knew from experience this would be where Met would scold him for fighting or lecture him in his behavior after the fight.

Met was silent as they walked in the direction of home. This bothered Ren even more. Perhaps she was exploring the possibilities of a much more effective punishment than a mere scolding. He muttered bits and pieces of after-thought retorts to Cal's foregone vocal threats. Without realizing it, he meant to provoke Met to deliver the scolding now in order to avoid any harsher punishment later. She continued in her silence, however. He proceeded with his mumblings of how he would 'fix him good' or 'next time I see him' until finally Met stopped. She did not turn her body to him, but looked down at his small face.

"Cal is your friend," she told him, pausing for a short time before walking again.

Normally Ren might have protested, objecting that certain actions negated the definition of a 'friend.' There was something in his older sister's expression, though. Something in the tone of her voice and her earnest, puzzled look when she said it. It caused him to reconsider his anger, and he felt almost ashamed at the hatred. He also fell silent as they walked.

The family gathering remained the same. The pre-planned menu consisted of a nutritionally balanced meal with little taste. Mother inquired dutifully about the children's daily studies. Father informed everyone about his completed tasks of the day. No one mentioned of Ren's 'incident' at play time. This was not within the normal parameters of their parental duties and was Met's responsibility. Mother and father's comments and inquiries were few and only came after a barely visible spark running quickly within their messengers. The messengers were fitted tightly onto their heads, leaving only the face exposed. A colorful array of soft, tentacle-like communication links spread generously and randomly over its surface, floating freely.

With the gathering completed, Ren pulled his study materials onto the table. He grudgingly punched up the area where he last finished. He took in a few lines and paused, watching his parents. After clearing the table of the used contents, they moved in perfect synchronicity to the holding area in the next room. Comfortably reclined, they attached the master link to their messengers. Momentarily, their eyes were closed and quick, colorfully bright sparks consumed the surface of their heads.

Ren wondered what it was like to be conformed, to have your thoughts, feelings and purpose delivered to you constantly. He often wanted to ask them, but knew they would not, or could not, answer. He would ask Met after her conformation. Perhaps she could tell him. Perhaps she would remember how it was before.

The darkness consumed the outside. Met looked into the night sky and took in the brilliant arrangement of stars. She knew most of the cluster's names and said them to herself as she looked at each one. She would know all of them after conformation. She would know a lot of things and she would never forget. She wondered if she would ever look at the stars again, though. None of the adult conformers ever did. There were many things they did not do. It was not something...necessary.

She walked into the living area with only a glimmering of light to lead her. She passed the entrance to the distant holding area and saw the bright illumination of her parents. They were asleep, she guessed. Ren's room flickered, half bathed in light. She walked to his entrance and stood against the opening. Ren lay in bed with his hands clasped behind his head, gazing upward in wonder. In the small space above him, a glowing set of rings hovered. Smoothly colored spheres raced along the path of the rings. In the center of this display, a larger sphere boiled in contortions of energy, representing their star. He commanded the orbits to move faster and faster until soon they were little more than a blur.

Met watched, smiling softly at the wonder in his large eyes. Met's eyes were different. Smaller, wiser and not always so easily filled with wonder anymore. They were deep with a dark blue outline and, in recent times, more prone to gaze beyond a subject. Her gaze often wandered into an area far away from their original focal point. She was very tall and her long, scarlet hair flowed in a beautifully straight line to her waist where it ended abruptly. It called forth the admiration of all of her peers even though it was customary to cut it shorter the closer you approached conformation.

"You are supposed to be asleep," she said lightly. "And your study materials are not intended for amusement."

Ren ended the orbital chaos.

"I didn't want to sleep. Will you tell me a story?"

She walked in and sat down, moving her hair over the front of her shoulder, combing it softly with her fingers.

"Will you go to sleep if I do?"

"I promise."

Met looked thoughtfully out of the opening on the side of his room. There were only faint lights visible from the other dwellings. Ren saw she was thinking of a story, trying to remember, or perhaps construct, an appropriate tale to delight her little brother into a world of dreams. Finally, she looked at him again, twisting her hair into temporary braids as she spoke.

"Once upon a time there was a land in the oceans no one ever knew about..."

Ren listened as the story unfolded, amazed at the wonderful places and people she told him of and awed by the incredible things they did. He did not believe she was manufacturing the story, but was sure he never heard it before. Could it be possible that she was able to arrange such an imaginary tale as she went? He did not know. Half way through the story he interrupted her.

"Are you going to miss it?"

She was startled, pulled out of the flow of her imaginary thoughts

"Going to miss what?" she asked, confused.

"Your hair. You fix it in so many different ways. You won't be able to do that anymore."

"I...I won't have to. Things will be different, Ren."

"What will it be like to change? Will it hurt?"

She let the braids in her hair go and the locks fell back into place.

"Ren," she said, "why are you so curious about the conformation? You have years before you are to conform. There is no reason for you to think of such things now."

"I want to know. What is it like to always know what you are to do? What is it like to have every answer to your questions?"

She looked again out of the opening before turning to her brother.

"Go to sleep, Ren. We will finish the rest of the story another time."

He pulled the covers tightly in protest, turning on his side and closing his eyes. Met watched his delicate face for a moment until his breathing became steadied by sleep. She went to the doorway and turned momentarily towards her little brother. For a brief instance, his beautiful innocence caused a pang of regret to pass through her. If only he could stay this way forever, forever young and never to worry of questions and deep concerns that only grow in you until conformation.

One day, Ren," she whispered. "You will have the answers to all of your questions.

Watcher Sela pulsed. The thoughts of at least a thousand danced through her intelligence. She watched, processing the information, gathering it into what would become eventual understanding. She was beginning to see now. The race of people below her was stagnant; not evolving. The change, the conformation each individual goes through gives them the direction they go in. It gives them the instructions to live. There is no need to reach for something more. There is no 'more'.

Watcher Sela considered the one called 'Met'. She was different. Her mind was continually occupied by the approaching day of her conformation. It was

Watcher Kenor who finally decided to observe the process of the conformation. Sela would closely follow Met until the day of change. Then they would continue on their journey.

Met stared blankly at the figure in front of the group. She sat, arms folded much the same as the others did. The speaker, the one they called Anon, spoke in meticulous monotone while the colorful lights flashed around his scalp. He explained the reasons for conformation and answered their questions. He persuaded the group their transition would be simple, painless and uneventful. It was necessary.

Their group consisted of eleven children participating in the ceremony to adulthood. Finally, this exciting time arrived. They were eager and smiled expectant smiles at one another. This was their time. Time to leave old thoughts behind and open the door to the infinite.

It was Met who echoed her brother's concerns, 'Will it hurt?' It was the only question she could think to ask. All of her life up to this point was filled with an over-abundance of questions, but this was all she could speak.

"It is most painless and simple," Anon answered after a brief flicker of light.

The group entered into the conformation structure by twos. Presently, Met saw a couple from her group return with their newly fitted messengers. Their heads flashed in brilliant colors and she knew they were receiving the answers to their many questions. One of them was Met's friend, Nealah. She nodded and smiled to Met as she exited the area just as she did towards the entire group. There was no excited greeting. No quick, hushed conversation to explain away the mystery. Nealah did not even pause to wish her friend well. Met watched her as she left. There were two more ahead of her and then it would be her turn.

The time was quickly approaching, rushing upon her like an unstoppable force. The others grew impatient, ready to receive the gift of adulthood. But she felt the pull of unanswered questions. So many questions and no time to ask them. The general feeling among her group was not one of caution. This was a time of celebration...a time of happiness. To ask any questions now was to admit a feeling of discontent and who was she to feel such a thing at her own conformation? It was happening too quickly for her, though. Rushed. She needed time to think, to understand what all of this really meant.

Eventually, two more exited the conformation chambers. Met watched them with their brilliant flashing. Looking into the eyes of the one to the left, there was something different. A hint of...disappointment almost. Maybe. But it disappeared as quickly as she saw it and was replaced by the pleasant look conformation always brought.

It was time now. Met and another entered the chamber together. Looking at the surroundings, she found it much less magical than her imaginations allowed her. A very small room with only a few half-height divisions greeted her. Its only rescue from complete blandness was a lattice work of transparent cables clinging permanently overhead. The multi-colors flashed ominously within them, traveling to a centralized location. The main receptacle, erected in the very center of the room, brought an end to the cables in the form of twin connectors. They hung loosely on either side where vertical slabs lay opposite one another. Met's eyes followed the flashing lights as they sprang from hidden sources and down to the end connectors. Nothing flashed out of the ends.

Two attendants greeted them and motioned them to their respective places. Met felt a slight shake of nervousness in her arms.

It's okay. It's alright. It is finally time.

Sitting in a comfortable chair, Met noticed the nearby horizontal slab. It was much like the upright ones in the middle of the chamber. Her attendant dutifully grasped the bulk of Met's long hair and burned it in half with her silent cutter. She continued by gathering together the remainder and sliced it in two parts. It was only now when Met glanced down at her fallen strands did she notice a floor cluttered with many shades of hair. She recognized the distinct rich-blue of her friend's former head dressing.

It continued. Shorter and shorter until finally Met could feel the tingle of the cutter near her scalp. Carefully and slowly, she brought her head upward, leaving the image of the floor's montage of locks, much of which now consisted of her own hair. She could feel wetness near her cheek. Crying? Sad? What was the reasoning behind this emotion at such a time? Only thoughts of confusion answered her now. Some part of her that wasn't preoccupied with emotions gave a preliminary comfort: It would not be long before she would no longer need to search for such answers. They would be provided almost instantaneously.

Prompted to the lying position on the horizontal slab, Met felt the coldness of the bed against her cleanly shaven scalp. Odd feeling. Next, smooth hands covered her head with an even smoother liquid substance. It was not cold, but comforting - tingling her senses into feeling as if there was something there other than baldness. Then there was. Carefully and expertly, the attendant fitted her subject with a messenger, sliding it into complete tightness. Her hands moved about the neck, fastening the end of the fitting below the chin in some unseen and permanent way.

Nervousness again. The unexpected fitting caused Met to forget the nice tingling sensation. She spoke without realizing she even wanted to. "I...will I remember things?"

The attendant looked at her, head cocked.

Met realized the vocalization came from her own lips and felt uneasy. The time for questions was over, but now she must at least make clear her question to the attendant. "I mean...simple things. Will I remember reading stories to my little brother?"

The attendant smiled her pleasant smile upon hearing the completed question, her own headset flashing continuously. "Why would you wish to remember such things?" was all she said.

Met did not have time to ponder the answer. The attendant had delivered it with such reassurance, such confidence. Why, indeed, would one want to remember those small things? Why, when an entire world would soon be opened up to her, to provide answers to all questions. Where was the reasoning in wishing to retain simple past memories when the combined knowledge of the entire race waited at the door?

The attendant guided her to the vertical slab. She somehow knew this was the final stage in her transcendence into adulthood. Standing flat against the cold surface, her guide positioned her head ever so slightly and instructed her to place her hands flat against the coldness. Then she saw a thin strap of material circumnavigating her eyesight. The attendant brought it completely around and fastened it to something on the slab. It was tight. Too tight. A sharp, stabbing pain entered her mind, causing her to gasp loudly.

The attendant calmed her with more soothing words and gave the indication that it would not be much longer. It was longer, however, and the pain was excruciating. She did not think she would survive the process. What was the purpose for this horrible pain? The only way to divert pain, she had learned over the years, was to concentrate on something, anything but physical discomforts. The only thoughts that came to her when she searched were those of Ren. Why did she keep thinking of those silly stories? Ren would soon learn to construct his own stories from imagination. Ren could live in worlds of imagination by himself, as she had often done, and he would be alright. It kept returning to her, though, amidst stabs of searing pain, the vision of her sitting at his bedside while her mind wandered and her mouth vocalized the journey.

Then she felt it. A flood of information streams pouring into her mind, disinterested at where their destinations lay. Knowledge. Pure, unabated and unforgiving knowledge washed into her being. It ran into her mind, painfully at first, but slowly getting better. Content, happy, grateful, joyful, good. Subservient.

For an instant, Ren was there somewhere. He was asking her about confirmation and what it was like. She could see herself answer him. "It is good."

Met reacted compulsively. She flung her hands upward, not really knowing how or why. She gripped handfuls of the many cables protruding from her head and pulled them with strength she didn't know she possessed. She felt the smaller ones give way and a strange crackling noise pierced her ears. The pain from the strap came back. She grasped more of the stringy mass and ripped them from their origins. In the process, the strap gave and the pain was gone. When she could find no more wires, the presence of a large umbilical cord restrained her from the back center of her head. She tried to push away from the slab, but the connection was too tight. She clawed at her headset, but it would not come loose. Using arms and legs, she pushed away with all her might until she heard a loud click and went flying forward, knocking down the curious attendant.

A numbing pain clouded her mind now. Her vision blurred and the entire area tipped dizzily. Struggling to her feet, she found herself unable to stand up straight. She saw the attendant's inquisitive face, her head cocked to one side and headset pulsing furiously. She said something. One word, but Met could not hear or understand. Hunched over, she made her way through the simple maze, swaying from side to side and kept her fluttering eyes on the entrance.

Once outside, the brightness of the day hurt her eyes. Her peers gathered beyond the holding area. She could see them turning to her, but could not distinguish their bland, confused faces. A fear enveloped her as the first hints of sane thought returned. She had committed a great wrong and some sort of punishment would be exacted upon her, though she could not imagine what it would be. Her mind raced with possible scenarios, possible youth-discipline methods, but none seemed to match her transgression. The more she thought, the more her dizzy mind became crowded with fear. As far as her knowledge reached, she knew of no single adult receiving any form of punishment for any single act. There was no precedence, but, she wasn't quite an adult now, was she?

The ground came up to meet her more than once. She stumbled, cutting her knee and adding to her wealth of pain. Who would deliver her punishment? The only beings respected as higher individuals were the preparers of conformation. However, this was merely an honorary position and though now she knew their process did inflict a level of pain, they did not have the authority or knowledge to judge her. To her, this meant only one thing. Her violations would be judged and her punishment enacted by the very creator that brought them all into existence.

The sheer terror of this thought gave her great strength and she ran, fighting the sickening dizziness to leave all that she knew behind. She fell hard. This time her entire leg did not want to move without sending unbearable pain to her senses. She struggled to her feet once more and tried to run. With each stride, a thousand impulses of torture shot into her.

She could feel the tears of hurt flowing from her eyes, but she ran.

Watcher Kenor consulted with the others for a short time. The crime was committed, it was decided, and the punishment must be enforced. Sela, the accused, pulsed a deep, harsh red. Jagged strips of her energy thoughts protruded from her form and into the others. She was not pleading or resisting, but persistent in her statement: She committed no wrong.

Kenor combined his being with the others. A large, fiery glow of boiling rainbow colors churned before Sela. Bolts of white-blue energy pierced her from the pulsing magistrate. The blinding strikes of information enlightened her of their verdict: She manipulated the simple being below. One of the thousands that were within her thoughts, she granted compassion (or was it experimentation) and changed the being's mind.

All of the watchers were dismayed by the condition of the stagnant race within their view. All understood that it was the order of things and it was a progression which would only change by their own doing. It was not the place of the watchers to inhibit or excite any form of change.

Sela allowed a simple thought to escape into the lower being's mind, however. A raised question. An altered consideration of right and wrong and the possible choices they contained. With her simple protrusion into one beings mind, she has changed a lifeform, possibly even a race of people, forever.

The punishment remained unstated by the glowing mass. There was only one. That of the complete annihilation of the accused. There was, however, a period of reform. A chance to retain, at least, a last claim of righteousness within her being. If only she would admit to the truth. Sela continued her exact statements into the mass without pause, draining the very energy from her life. Her claims insisted that it was by no interference from her that the being deviated from this world's long held ritual. That, for whatever reason, a strong curiosity prevailed within her consciousness. A will beyond the confines of her environment drove her in a direction far from that of what was expected. She chose her own destiny. *She chose her own destiny.*

The combined entity that was mainly Kenor watched as Sela drained herself, repeating her declarations. He would not let her continue this painful form of ending and so began the punishment. Their jagged connections with Sela became soft and smooth, uniform and humming until she was gone.

Cool water ran gently under Met's tormented body. When at last a taste of the salty liquid reached the level of her mouth, she coughed and forced herself back to consciousness. She raised her weary head slowly and looked out upon the blue horizon. Her squinting eyes blinked at the shining ocean waters before her.

Looking down, she took inventory of her body that lay sprawled upon the beach. She struggled to her hands and knees and crawled a small distance away from the approaching water, propping herself upon a great rock. Retrieving full consciousness and realizing she felt little pain, she allowed her eyes to widen at the infinite view before her.

This place was a memory. Her and other small ones were taken here long ago. They were given the view of the ocean, the same view that completely surrounded the land that was their world. They were taken there sometime after being informed of its existence. This was the barrier. This was the end of their habitation and the epitome of uselessness. They were taken to satisfy their simple, young curiosities and told never to return. Met never did until now and she could not even remember how she arrived. Another crime to add to her eventual punishment in whatever form it may present itself.

She stared in amazement at the distant rolling waves and the strangely calm, crashing sound they made. For a moment, she was also calm and wished her punishment would appear. But the memory of her outrage returned suddenly and startled her. Using the rock as leverage, she pulled herself to her feet, realizing a constant pain in her leg. As she stood, a lesser degree of the earlier dizziness also returned, delivering with it a sickening feeling.

She looked around, feeling what was left of the tentacles that protruded from her headset. She thought for answers, but none arrived. This gave her a strange sense of relief that she did not understand. There was the great ocean in front of her, the forest and mountains at her back and the empty sky above her. How could she find her way home? What punishment would await her if she returned? What would Ren think of her now? There were no answers.

She turned to the forest, unconsciously deciding it would be her next direction. Her eyes suddenly focused on something...someone standing not far from her. She wanted to be frightened, but oddly the fear evaded her, as if it had been temporarily used up due to her previous bouts with it.

There before her stood a giant more than twice her height. His ragged garments clung loosely without color. The top of his hairless crown was scarred with blotchy, red spots. The entire area where his left eye should reside was sunken in and smooth. His body was dirty and a yellowish grimy substance glistened from his knees down. He stood completely still, staring at Met with a horrified, round eye and an open mouth of imperfect and missing teeth.

The questions poured into Met's mind and amplified as the creature began walking towards her. Then, at last she arrived at the solution. This was the punishment due her. Her ill-doings would finally be rectified and she could rest at last. She gasped when its large, gritty arm clamped onto her own slender one. It pulled her easily and she fell, being dragged helplessly over the occasional rocks that plagued the beach. With great effort, she used the giant's arm and struggled to her feet, painfully attempting to match his stride to keep from falling again.

After some distance through the forest and into the area of great mountains, she at last succumbed to the strain and was again dragged. She felt sharp edges tear into her and small trees scrape her skin. When the giant proceeded through a particularly rocky terrain, she felt herself fading away again. Her entire body was in pain until pain was the norm. In her blurry, dismal thoughts, she considered it an effective punishment.

After an eternity, her uncaring companion came to a sudden stop. Turning his head so that his non-existent eye looked down upon her, he grunted. Then he slung her easily into the deep hole in front of him.

Ren's tears and antics did not aid him in his quest for information. Met was gone. This was her great day, the day of her conformation and she would come home and he would see his new sister, suddenly an adult. She never came. He heard the confusing stories from younger ones. They said she refused the change, others said she was killed by the transformation and still others said she ran away. Now, his mother stared down upon him with a knowing, constructed smile. Ren knew from experience that anything other than pure fact would not be offered from his parents. They were not concerned about the disappearance of their only daughter, but he did not know who else to ask.

"Leeta, your new caregiver, will be here soon. She will watch over your needs," his mother explained dutifully.

He looked up at this parent, his eyes glassy in a way she was no longer capable of. His mother was one of his providers. One who made provisions for the nourishment, saw to his basic needs and listened to his every question in order to supply flawless answers. She would go away for a time to perform the daily tasks that maintained their sustenance. His father's duties mirrored that of his mother's and all of their functions constantly alternated between the two. It was her turn to provide answers to Ren's never-ending inquiries as his father sat in perfect recline, attached to the master link.

The only answer was that his new attendant would be with him soon. Leeta was one of Met's friends, he remembered. She was slightly younger, though, and would not yet be conformed. She would see to the necessary development of Ren his parents could not perform. The exploration of his emotions, the expansion of his imagination and the cultivation of his creativity. With this development and with time, he would also be ready for conformation.

He slowly turned away from his mother's constant gaze. She was always with an answer, but without answer. He walked into his room, climbed onto the bed and thought about Met. He tried, without success, to remember any one of the stories she used to read him.

Kenor, once again a single entity, gave attention to the dilemma surrounding his group of watchers. The decision making process that he was now forced into was not a pleasant one. He must now discover the correct path that would eradicate Sela's mistake. It must be as it was before. It must follow as if they were never there. The procedure to reverse such ill effects, if it ever became necessary, was to take action as quickly as possible. For, as their elders undoubtedly knew from past wisdoms, the longer a wrong path is taken, the more the damage becomes permanently irreparable. It was now necessary for just such a reversal of events. Kenor did not have enough facts, however. Not about the action itself, but about the culture below. He decided to deviate from the procedure and gather more data in order to perform a correct reversal. If he acted too swiftly without the knowledge, he could allow the wrong to branch out to more wrong. He watched and waited.

Met's eyes fluttered open, seeing a small hole of light high above her. She lay still on her back for a second, allowing for a short contemplation of past events. Then, she decided to get up and explore her new, half-lit world. When she tried to move, however, she felt an incapacitating pain creak through her entire body. Although the younger ones sometimes broke limbs, she never did. Now she believed that every connection inside her must be dislodged or broken. She lay still another moment, letting her mind absorb the hurt. Expecting the next level of pain, she rolled over and observed the surroundings.

She lay in the center of a circular area with large entrances to tunnels stretching out in all directions. They were all dark except for the one directly in front of her, which contained a zig-zag pattern of occasional torches of light. She stared down the infinite passage, trying to focus on the end. Looking back up to the small hole above, she realized the impossibility of it being a means of escape.

The long, torch lit tunnel also appeared impossible in her current state of being. Resolving to give in to the pain and fatigue, she brought her head to rest on an outstretched arm. Then, a faraway noise captured her attention. She squinted, her eyes straining to see into the tunnel until she saw something moving. It came closer and the sound of steady footsteps grew louder. At first, it was odd in shape, almost imaginary as she tried to discern the figure at a great distance. Then, with horror creeping into her senses, she recognized it. The giant returned, hunched over to facilitate his outlandish height inside the tunnel. She gasped and tried to scramble to one of the other dark tunnels, but her body would not respond and the pain was too great. For the first time in her life, she screamed in fear as it grabbed her arm, once again dragging her.

In full stride, the thing pulled her into the entrance of the lighted tunnel. The uneven surface was full of rocks that would otherwise be smooth if one were not raked over them. Within a short distance, her eyes rolled upward to again see a strong, muscle-defined arm. From the large hand that locked onto her tiny wrist, it stretched into his broad shoulder and completed their inseparable connection. It was the last thing she saw before darkness claimed her.

The giant stopped, turned his one eye upon her unmoving form and cocked his head in curiosity. He let out a small grunt and pulled her easily over his ample back, hunching even lower as he continued through the tunnel.

It was first the unrecognizable odor and then the sound of forced breathing that greeted Met's return to consciousness. When her exhausted eyes adjusted to the soft light, the vision that hovered over her caused an abrupt motion of fear. A face of a thousand wrinkles peered at her through old, watery eyes. An enlarged headset crowned the sullen profile with hundreds of small tentacles flowing freely in all directions. There were no brilliant, randomized flashes, but rather a dull, white glow that slowly crawled around its curved surface. A shaky arm moved a sharp instrument towards her scalp.

She caught his wrist smartly and felt her own arm trembling as she stopped him.

Aged eyes floated in the direction of her gaze.

"It is quite amazing you are alive."

"Whatever my punishment, I wish to remain that way," she said, realizing a dryness in her throat.

"You have been severed from the master link prematurely. I must attend the wound if you are to continue to survive."

She stared at the sharp object twitching haphazardly between his fingers.

"If I intended to kill you," his voice crackled, "I could easily have accomplished that before you awoke. I will attend to your damage."

Her gaze shifted back to him and her eye lids closed partially, brought on by a temporary loss of any and all strength or will. Her grip loosened from his wrist and she allowed her arm to return slowly to her side. He hesitated, watching her dazed expression and then proceeded to the center of her head.

A falling sensation enveloped Met as she journeyed into a dream world. She was flying now with vibrant colors surrounding her, guiding her. Moving swiftly, she saw her world below as the peaceful harmony it was. The outline of her home became clear and she flew down towards it, catching glimpses of other dwellers as they walked. She floated inside and hovered, looking down upon her family. Everyone, including herself, was gathered and seated. They were all playing one of Ren's silly games. Her parents laughed with them, something she had never heard them do.

She watched curiously for a time, but then she was in flight once again, streaming gloriously into a great light in the sky. It did not hurt her eyes as she stared into its beauty and she felt its warmth upon her skin. She turned in mid-air and spread colorful wings she didn't know she had. She watched the great brightness as it grew more and more immense. Suddenly her wings dissolved and the new-found peacefulness fled her body. She came back to reality with the old one looming over her with some sort of portable bright illumination. He turned it off.

"You will heal completely with time, but you shouldn't continue to experience any of the dizziness that you most likely had."

She made an effort to lift her head up, intending to survey her surroundings, but found it too painful.

"I have also tended to your other wounds," the old one continued. "I must apologize for Klazen," he waved indication across the area to where the giant stood tall and motionless. "He sometimes collects things for me and thought it would please me to bring you here."

This time she successfully lifted her head up, observing the space she found herself in. The area was large enough to be a dwelling, but not like any she ever saw. She was quite sure she was still inside one of the great mountains. The illumination was also much like that which she was accustomed to. At the far end of the low slab she lay on, was a large, pulsing object. The top of its rectangular form contained a sphere of some type of visible energy flowing outward from within the center. The pulsing and energy tentacles were in unison with those that emanated from her captor.

"Where am I?" She brought her head carefully back down.

"You are within a mountain that is infested with a myriad of caves and tunnels...left behind by a civilization of long ago. You are in my dwelling."

At once, she did not believe him. She knew, as she was taught, that there were no other civilizations. There was only one, the one that existed now, which was created from the higher beings.

He brought his hands to his chest and Met noticed for the first time he was not standing. He appeared to be confined to his seat, which floated barely above the floor.

"I am Zear," he said tiredly, anticipating her next question. "Why did you not complete the conformation? Was there a malfunction in the process?"

Met turned on her side and pulled herself up to sit on the slab and felt nervousness combine with her pain.

"I...I rejected the conformation. I do not know why, but I could not allow myself to..."

An otherwise old, expressionless face rearranged its wrinkles into visible surprise and disbelief.

"You rejected? Impossible!"

His emotions seemed to come from within rather than supplied by some outer instruction. Yet, he appeared to be older than any she had ever known. She looked up at his flowing tentacles.

"You are...conformed?"

He laughed and coughed deeply before smiling at her.

"Of course I am conformed. But not like your friends out there. I am conformed to that great provider of life." He motioned to the pulsing rectangle. "I have been long dead, but it delivers to me every impulse that continues my life functions. At first, it was an amazing achievement. To live beyond that which time has set aside for you. Now," he lifted his eyes up to the apparatus, "now, I haven't the courage to turn it off."

She looked at him strangely.

"Why would you wish to end?"

"There comes a point in your life when there is no longer meaning, no longer the excitement of discovery. It is indeed possible to live...too long."

Met felt an ache in her head and put her hand to her forehead, allowing her fingers to divide some of her inactive tentacles. She could not quite relate to what the old one was saying. Not many in her world lived to obtain wrinkles and none lived longer than necessary, reaching death when instructed by the conformation.

"I could remove that for you," the old one said, shaking a finger at her headset, "but your scalp would look similar to Klazen's."

She flashed a quick glance at the giant, whom she still held fear for, and back to the old one. She shook her head almost politely. "You said your name is Zear, but I have never heard of you. Why do you stay here? Why do you not live as the others?"

He floated slowly over to a table cluttered with mechanical things Met had never seen the like of and began fidgeting with one of the objects. His back was turned and it seemed that he would ignore her question. Finally, his attention still immersed within the device he held, he answered her. "I used to live among your people. Long ago. Things were much different then. There was so much against us. Disease, war, hunger..."

"I am not sure what those words mean."

Zear tossed the object upon the table in exchange for another one, his hands shaking. He half-turned to his visitor.

"Exactly," he chuckled. "That was the point of the conformation. So that no one should know such ills of society. To take away those mental processes that contributes to such things and substitutes them with pure knowledge. The allowance for purified research into medicine came into existence as a direct result. I predicted that, also. What I did not predict, however, was the subtle elimination of other thought processes as an eventual side effect of our newly conformed society." He frowned, examining yet another object. "Things such as individuality, the will to choose and freedom became dim within every conformed mind. But I don't suppose you know the meaning of those words, either." He turned to her momentarily to confirm his suspicions. "I didn't think so. It doesn't really matter if you understand them or not, you know. They live in the younger ones, if only for a short time."

Met stood up, ignoring the various aches in her body.

"I...chose not to be conformed. I was wrong."

Zear rotated his chair in her direction and shifted his eyes up to her.

"You did no wrong. If, indeed, you made the choice, it doesn't matter what the choice was, it was the right one. It was right simply because you made it."

She shook her head.

"I will be punished."

"You will not be punished. There are no provisions for punishment within the system. The young are not punished unless they receive it from those not yet conformed that tend them. The older are not punished because they are conformed and, being conformed, they will not commit any act that requires punishment. Don't you see? It's the perfect system, the solution to the problems that plagued our entire race."

Met rubbed her left shoulder, feeling a temporary flash of pain. She sat back down upon the slab, trying to comprehend what the old one was saying.

Zear rotated back to the table.

"If it were not completely necessary, perhaps the conformation could be ended," he said, wearily. "Many things that should have ended long ago are past due. Perhaps your rejection is the beginning of things to come."

"It was a mistake," she admitted. "I was only thinking of my small brother and of past memories that would no longer be of any need."

"You will come to realize, as I have, that memories are more important, the older you get. It is the conformation that is wrong, but as I have said, ultimately necessary."

She looked at him sharply. A sudden, defensive anger filled her voice, but she did not know why.

"If the conformation is wrong, then why does it continue? Why do the higher ones not devise a better way for us to live?"

Zear continued his work, the slow crawl within his headset remaining unchanged. "It will continue because the higher ones have no conscious to change it. It will continue because the very system that is in place is designed to perpetuate itself. Those of the conformed that are designated to instruct in the purpose and necessity of conformation will see to it. They see to it through consistent orders from the system and no one can change the system. It will continue...unless there were suddenly many such as yourself who choose not to conform.

"And that is very unlikely. Since the very beginning of the conformation, there have only been two who have denied the process. You and Klazen...and the only reason Klazen rejected is because his limited mind could not handle the messenger. He would have died also had I not been nearby. He has stayed with me since.

"I know you cannot possibly begin to understand, but the process of continually receiving instructions on how one must live life is contrary to what is meant to be. It is only necessary because we have made it to be that way...to live in an orderly manner."

Met looked upon the dirty surface of the old one's home.

"If it were not this way, all would be as the younger ones. All would need to be tended."

"Yes," Zear said, nodding his head slowly, "they would. Just as before."

"How do you know all of this...of conformation? And why do you grow so old as to wish to die?"

Zear replaced the strange object to its original spot on the table and looked down upon his shaking, wrinkled hands.

He said, "You must rest now if you are to recover."

Kenor pulsed a soft red. The thoughts of Met and only ten others resided in his multi-accommodating consciousness. He could see the thoughts of the others and made the necessary observations, but it was those that radiated from Met that commanded his full attention now. More than listening, he was searching. Combing her nervous path-ways, he sought to completely re-construct the moment of contamination.

If he could find the exact branches of the disaster and could eradicate them, he may yet be able to solve the dilemma. This way, the one known as Met could live and her only repercussions would be some memory loss. Otherwise, he would have to destroy her and that was something he wished to avoid. He was pleased to realize, however, others in her surrounding culture remained uninfected by this defilement. It was the first time he saw any advantage to their stagnate civilization, though the advantage was purely his.

He probed into her thoughts, into her memory as she remained unaware of even the slightest presence. She twisted and turned in her sleep, but only due to nightmarish visions of her recent adventures. Kenor soared at immense speeds though her intertwining network of memory, discovering alien images. He saw visions both recent and old, a wealth of which Met had long ago abandoned. He encountered childhood fears, unexplained violence among her companions, the constant guidance of her one-time tender, Yenalla. He discovered a world of impressions etched upon her mind like the markings of ancient civilizations found in stone. Then there were the continuous and ever-changing aspects of her being. Those of fear, happiness, and content coupled with a thirst for knowledge and understanding and...an undying curiosity.

Kenor stopped at the turning point. The point known to these beings as conformation. The point where Sela was to simply suggest another path, but he was hesitant. It was not a normal process to travel a consciousness in this manner. They were merely watchers and did not delve too deeply into any of their subject's minds. It allowed them to monitor so many at once.

Only in these circumstances was it necessary, when their own intrusions and misjudgments demanded rectification. He hesitated. Having sifted through her entire life, finding things even she would never again have need of or even recognize, he comprehended all of her. Everything that she was or did in her past lay the groundwork for all that she would become. He floated at the turning point, feeling a cloud of understanding and fear envelope him for the first time on his voyage. He knew what information waited before him.

He ventured on, examining the sparks of memory carefully as he progressed. He boldly glided down the path-ways, grasping at all available data and branching out to every possibility that sparked from the very moment she resisted her conformation. He combed deeper, quickening his pace and searched frantically within layer after layer of memories and knowledge. Even so, Sela's influence was nowhere to be found.

Leeta finally left the room. Ren successfully convinced her that the story she told him lulled him to sleep. He lay in the darkness now and felt a single droplet of water run down from his eye.

A child's emotion, he thought. I am older now, I am grown. No one else can find her, but I can. I must.

He lay still for a moment, contemplating the consequences of whatever actions he was about to take. Any discipline would come from Leeta. Leeta. The one that must read her stories from books for lack of an imagination. The one that has no true desire to see Ren develop into something greater than what he now was. Leeta, he observed, already had a younger one to tend to and so will only guide Ren because the responsibility has fallen to her, not because it is something she desired to do.

He climbed silently out of the round opening in his room and into the night. No one ever went out at night and the darkness frightened him, but he concentrated on his direction. He made his way past dark dwellings and through eerie shadows which the night sky cast upon him. He felt his bare feet dip into the cool, clean sand with every step, aiding him on his silent journey.

At last, he came upon the gulf of space that separated the dwellings from his destination. He hastily bridged the distance through the sand, sprinting from right to left as if he were avoiding traps along the way. His breath tolled in gasps, he leaned hard upon the surface of a very smooth wall and looked around the corner.

The majestic outline of the conformation structure greeted his vision and he shivered with anticipation. He examined the landscape for a moment, allowing his breath to return. Then, he slowly ascended the steps, contemplating the artistic designs upon columns that stood on both sides. He looked ahead, pondering the concentric circles that decorated the front of the complex. He wondered why none of the dwellings were this beautiful.

The double opening loomed before him. He approached, feeling tiny shocks of fear echo throughout his body. He pushed at the opening with no success. Then he pounded, lightly at first, and heard the shallow sounds reverberate inside. Pausing, he glanced up at the tall entrance, feeling a sort of betrayal. No doors had ever denied him before.

He pulled, pounded and kicked the unmoving access, feeling anger replace his fears. He continued in his rage until he felt the pain of scrapes upon his hands and feet and the bleariness of tears cloud his vision. In a last, desperate attempt, he slammed his hands flatly against the surface to no avail. Slowly, he guided himself against the wall to a nearby corner. An artistic crevice provided an escape for his defeat and he slunk pitifully within it, resting his head upon bent knees.

There was an exciting development upon the world below and the watchers eagerly took in every second. Kenor, however, gave into their past desire to move on even though these wishes were no longer valid. Not entirely his decision, it applied to any area where contamination had spawned and rectification completed. Neither had truly happened in this case, but the past actions dictated the response. They would go.

In these last moments, his form flowed freely within his chambers, each particle of his being softly pulsing remembrances of Sela. There was a wrong committed here, a consequence of hasty judgment. If a world could deprive stagnation in a single instance of rejection, then perhaps there was hope for him also. It would be quite interesting to see what events perpetuated from this instance. He would like to watch and learn someday…if they were ever allowed to return to this place and time.

A collection of days passed as Met slowly recovered. During this time she learned more from the old one. Many of the concepts he spoke of were strange, but he showed her a library of storage that held all the previous knowledge of their world. The information could be retrieved by placing a curious band around the forehead. Then, all she had to do was select from hundreds of topics stored in little spheres. The information poured into her mind. Much of it was alien to her and the concepts were difficult. But slowly, she began to piece some things together. There was so much that she thought at first were fantasy stories. There were horrifying things that she felt could not possibly be true. As she devoured the fragments of history, however, her open mind began to see glimpses of a larger picture. She began to feel very small.

Zear lay still on the horizontal slab that once facilitated Met's recovery. His old eyes focused on the curved texture of the cave's ceiling for the first time. He followed lines of cracks and crevices until they disappeared out of his peripheral and allowed a wrinkled smile of content to fall upon his lips.

"Destroy the machine, now. I am ready."

Met walked up next to the slab, holding a long, slender object with both hands. The object was smooth and shiny and was unlike any material she had ever known. She held it with purpose.

"This will complete your life," she said. You will end. Do you understand what you ask of me?"

"Of course," came the labored reply. "Once it is done, Klazen will lead you out. That is my wish. That is our agreement."

"But Klazen could..."

"Klazen cannot harm me," the old one replied wearily. "He has protected me all this time. I saved his life and he will not take mine."

Met walked to the end of the slab and considered the colorful lights that somehow prolonged his endurance. She took a few steps back and leveraged her body, raising the heavy object. She hesitated for a second, shifting her eyes to the old one on the slab. He nodded his head ever so slightly without looking at her.

She brought the shiny pole forward and slammed it hard into the machine. It crackled and sparked. Klazen looked on from his corner, still and not understanding. She did it again and again, smashing the sphere into pieces. At last, a small bit of smoke and a steady crackling noise was all that emitted from it.

She dropped the object at her feet and knelt beside the slab. The steady crawl that once moved in the old one's head was still.

"It is done," he gasped. "When you are ready to leave, tell Klazen to 'get water'. He will take you to a place near your dwellings."

She watched as his breathing became more and more difficult and all the pain that he once evaded crept into his expression. "Why did you wish to end?" she asked.

"All things must end...you understand? All things. But the conformation must continue. It protects us from ourselves."

She shook her head.

"It must end, also. I can see that now. If anyone is to choose as I have, they must be given the chance to do so. I will end it."

He mustered a coughing laugh until he realized it was too painful.

"You cannot end it. There is only one who could have ended it and that is its creator. And I, its creator," he gasped a final breath, "chose not to."

Zear's eyes became still along with the rest of him. Met stood up, the horror of what he said invading her thoughts. She looked at the silent bulk of machinery that once provided life and then at the giant, whose expression was empty even now.

"No!" She cried and lifted the old one's body from the slab. She pulled him to the only tunnel opening and turned to the giant. "Klazen, get water".

Klazen turned to her, his disfigured face forming an expression of curiosity. Then, he strode past her and walked into the tunnel. She followed, heaving the old man's dead form with all of her strength. After a time, her pace slowed and she could not carry the weight. The giant was far into the long tunnel and soon would be gone from sight.

"Klazen," she called. He did not stop. "Klazen...help me."

The giant stopped, turned and returned to Met's location. Again, he offered the same look of curiosity, but grasped one of Zear's arms and pulled, not unlike he had pulled Met before. At first, she tried to help him, but was too slow for his stride and ended up running behind him.

They were not very far into the tunnel when Klazen turned left into an adjoining cave. It was very dark and Met had to keep from stumbling upon crude steps that pushed them upward. Before long, they encountered an intruding brightness and were suddenly on the surface. Without hesitation, the giant proceeded ahead, never looking behind and never slowing.

Finally, he stopped before a small stream of water and let Zear fall gently to the ground. He produced an odd-shaped container from somewhere within his rags and submerged it in the stream.

Met could see familiar outlines beyond the forest. The sight of low-ridged dwellings protruded at intervals though the thickness. Once again, she hauled Zear up to her, realizing that the giant would go no further. Klazen stood up, hid the filled container and watched her as she began to drag him off.

She stopped momentarily and turned back to the giant.

"He is gone, Klazen. You can no longer help him. You must help yourself now."

The giant stood still by the stream and watched as Met pulled Zear into the brush and out of sight. He stood there for a long time looking into the brush. Finally, he turned back into the direction he came and walked slowly away.

Met grunted as she struggled with Zear's body. She tried to lift him over her back, but could not. At last, she found herself trudging through the familiar sands of home. It was at least mid-day and several traveling dwellers dotted the terrain. Upon seeing Met and her strange hindrance, they would cock their heads momentarily and go along their way.

She pulled him through the sand, gasping for strength. Eventually, she stumbled and they both went down, coming to rest on a hard, shiny surface. She looked up at the familiar designs of the conformation structure. Clambering to her feet, she found a renewed energy and pulled Zear into the conformation chamber and onto an awaiting slab. She looked around, noticing that whatever damage she may have inflicted upon the chamber was either very minimal or had been repaired. An attendant appeared by her side.

"You are not to be conformed this day."

"No," she said in measured breaths, "this one is to be conformed. Prepare him." She pointed at the unmoving form.

The attendant looked down upon Zear, her messenger alive with colorful sparks.

"This one has ended. He cannot be conformed."

"Prepare him. Prepare him now," she insisted.

The attendant looked at her blankly and, after receiving a flickering of information, went to work upon Zear's scalp. Using a device similar to the hair remover, she cut away the odd apparatus that adhered to his head, pulling off pieces of skin with it. Next, she covered the newly exposed area with the smooth liquid and dutifully fit him with a skin-tight messenger.

"That is all I can do," she said.

"Finish him. Make him conformed," Met demanded.

The attendant took a few steps back.

"That is all I can do."

Met grabbed Zear from the slab and pulled him up to the vertical station, feeling one of the joints snap in his arm. She held him up by the neck and pulled the restrainers around him, holding him in place. Reaching up to the large, dangling cable, she pulled it down and clicked it into place on his messenger. She watched as the colorful flow of information lit up his headset.

The attendant came out of seclusion.

"It cannot work that way. This is the way." She took control of the system and went through the normal procedures, applying her skill to the controls as if she were training someone.

Suddenly, Zear's eyelids fluttered and his lips twitched. He opened his eyes and, though they were darting wildly, he recognized where he was.

"What have you done?" his voice was barely audible.

"You have taken the place of the next to be conformed," Met said. "No doubt, the system will keep you alive well into that person's adulthood."

"Why have you done this? He gasped. "Please...release me."

"Release yourself," she said, angrily." Shut down the system and end it."

"I cannot..."

"Then you will live. You have a choice."

"Please," he begged, his eyes trying to focus on her, "the pain is unbearable."

"End it. End it so that all may choose as I have. It will end your pain as well."

His erratic breathing slowed and his body became still. He looked at her with watery eyes. "You do not understand," he said. "I chose not to end it long ago. There was a time when it could be stopped, but that time has passed. It cannot be stopped."

She looked at him through her own glassy eyes, shaking her head.

"There must be a way," she said, choking back the urge to cry.

"Please," he said gently. "Please release me."

She looked at his aged face with all its wrinkles that time had rewarded him with. She thought of him living all of those years in isolation with only the silent giant, Klazen as his companion. Although he looked calm now, she could see the pain etched into his face and evident in his eyes. She thought perhaps he deserved this punishment of pain. Then she thought that perhaps no one deserves such pain. As she looked at him, she carefully moved her hands around the master link connection. The look in his eyes changed ever so slightly and she could see a mixture of gratitude and remorse in them. She removed the link that was keeping him alive.

Met slowly sank to the floor and sat against the slab. She looked around as if in a haze, feeling lost and alone. Finally, she put her head down. A myriad of emotions swirled within her, but on top of it all was the sinking feeling of defeat. For a brief moment, she thought about the instance when she was connected to the system. Compared to what she was feeling now, it had been a colorless void. It was an apathetic state of existence with no worry, no fear and no hatred. But it was also with no true happiness, no desire and no love. Her parents were living in that void now just as all adults were. Just as Ren would be someday.

The room came back into focus and as she stared straight ahead, she felt an unknown fury burn its way through her being. It culminated in the determination that now shone in her eyes. She stood up and looked around the room, at last seeing the attendant who had her head cocked in some perpetual loop of confusion. Met had completely forgot she was there.

"Do you require assistance?" The attendant asked.

"Get out."

"You are not authorized to –"

"I said get out," Met said, shoving the woman towards the doorway.

The attendant stumbled a bit, straightened and slowly continued towards the doorway. Her messenger was alive with pulsing lights, but the confusion did not leave her face.

Met looked up at the clear cables that hung from above. She turned back to where the lifeless Zear was strapped to the slab. She grasped the master link above his head and pulled on it with all her might. At first the tube only stretched a little, but as she grunted and pulled, something broke loose from above and a mass of cable came spiraling to the floor.

She did the same for the other master link and moved quickly to one of the panels the attendant had used. She ripped it from its enclosure and started smashing it against the slab. As pieces flew to the floor, she looked around for other things in the large room. She destroyed the remaining panels and, finding nothing else, she went to one of the horizontal slabs and tried to lift it. She grunted and tried with all her strength, but the thing seemed to be unmovable. She kicked at it several times, but it remained solid. Then she slammed her arm down upon its surface and yelled in pain. Stretching her arms across the top of it, she tried to pull it from the other side and screamed in frustration when it would not budge.

She allowed herself to collapse, her arms still stretched across the slab. She felt that same feeling of defeat as it crept its way into her, but her anger pushed it back. Suddenly, she realized the doorway had become blocked. She shifted her focus to it and could not believe her eyes.

Klazen.

The giant stood there, much like he had when she first saw him. In fact, for a brief instance Met felt that same fear from their first encounter. However, it was immediately followed by a strange joy in seeing him. Then, she frowned and looked over to Zear's lifeless body still strapped to the vertical slab. She wasn't sure if the giant had come back to find its only companion or because Met was the only one it knew now.

She walked over to the vertical slab, carefully removed the straps and pulled Zear's body into her arms. She walked to the entrance and stood in front of Klazen. The giant slowly approached her and looked at the lifeless form she was carrying. He gently brushed a large finger across Zear's face and let out a single moan of agony.

"I know, my friend," she said. "I know."

Met gestured towards the large conformation room and said, "Klazen...destroy."

Violent waves crashed onto the beach. Met stood, gazing serenely out at the deep blue waters. A short distance away, Klazen stood also, calmly facing the sea. On the beach, Ren was drawing imaginative creations in the sand.

"Where did you go?" Ren asked. Did you come here?"

Met smiled. "Yes, but not only here. It was an adventure that I will tell you about someday."

"I tried to find you. I tried to get inside that place but couldn't. I guess...I guess I fell asleep," he said, disappointedly.

Met's eyes softened. "You came to find me?"

"I was afraid. I thought they took you away."

"Ren, who would take me away?"

"The Watchers. The ones in your story, remember?"

"Oh," Met said with a small laugh. "I remember. No, no one took me away."

Ren frowned. "Why do our parents act so strange now? Why do all the older ones act strangely?"

Met laughed again.

"Because they are normal," she said. "They don't realize it yet, but they are normal." She looked over at her smaller brother, but he was already occupying his lack of attention by continuing his artistic gestures in the sand. "Ren," she began, "the coming times will not be easy. We have a great struggle ahead of us all."

He looked up at her, smiled and continued his creation in the sand.

Author's note: There was a local artist that used to sell his masterpieces at a nearby flea market. Occasionally, my wife and I would buy his artwork and one day, I picked up one that immediately inspired me. It was a rendition of a young woman with a scalp-fitting headdress on. Within her skullcap were intricate pieces of gadgetry and various other designs. Her head was lifted slightly upward and her gaze showed a kind of wisdom and determination. In an instant, it seemed, the entire story came to me. I only had to work out the details. She is, hopefully, one of the strongest characters I have written.

In A Perfect World

Dager saw Casillya in his dreams again. His mental journey brought him to a bright place filled with lavish marble furnishings. Long, endless hallways faced him at every turn. Perfect paintings, artistic expressions from some long forgotten era, decorated the walls. The cleanliness of the place was a nagging reminder he must still be asleep and this place was only a creation of the mind. Still, the subconscious part of him wondered if this was real and it caused the dream to persist. He ran aimlessly down infinite corridors, searching in vain and feeling the frustration and fear welling up from within. He knew there were others -- hundreds, maybe thousands -- searching just as he was. He had to find her first. Frantic, he moved faster and faster, forcing open doors to empty spaces, his heart pounding hard as he passed through large empty rooms. There was nothing but emptiness here in this maze of perfect architecture.

Exhausted, he leaned heavily against a nearby wall, feeling the pounding of his heart in his chest echoing through his head. Just around the corner was another hallway. He slid his body along the wall towards the corner, not having the energy to go on. As expected, it was just another passageway stretching on forever, with no end in sight. Unlike the other hallways he passed, this one hurt his eyes. Instead of seeing the walls closing in to nothingness, his eyes blurred when he tried to look to the end. He squinted, straining to make the image clearer, but his eyes felt white hot with pain. Then suddenly, as if a dense fog had been lifted from his burning eyes, he could see in perfect clarity. There, at the end of the corridor, she sat in a large circular room. A lovely variety of plants, trees and flowers turned the room into an oasis. In the center of it all, a crystal clear fountain provided three wonderful geysers. They pushed their way upward three meters into the air until it was impossible to go on, succumbing to gravity and falling back over themselves in tiny separations of clean, beautiful water.

She sat on the marble edge of the fountain clothed in white satin. She was beautiful, of course. Her long, brown hair flowed down one side of her shoulder. Silently and without motion, she gazed into the stream. The sheer radiance of her face with all its peacefulness made the beautiful surroundings pale in comparison.

Dager watched as if he stood beside her, yet knowing he was far down the distant corridor. He watched as she slowly reached to the pool and waved her hand across the surface. She brought up an outstretched hand to him and smiled. He could not take his eyes off her face. Never in his life had he seen anyone -- or anything -- so beautiful. Her amber eyes shone deep with honesty and a peacefulness sweeping over him. All his inhibitions broke down. The hatred in his heart vanished and all of the pain, hunger, violence, and rage within melted away and he felt tears stream down from his burning eyes. When at last he was able to break her sincere gaze, his eyes followed her arm down to her outstretched hand. In her palm she offered a small pool of clean water, but his eyes moved quickly back to her wrist. There he found the final proof of her identification. No doubt this was her. The beautiful amber eyes and stunning perfection was all he really needed to be sure, but the symbol on her wrist left no doubt. The symbol depicted the earth bathed in rays of sunlight. Rays of hope.

He looked into her eyes again, feeling the last bit of animosity drain from his soul. He felt as if her face was close to his. She moved the water towards his lips.

"They're coming," she said.

He flew backwards down the endless hallway, away from her at impossible speed and found himself still peering around the corner, his heartbeat once again thundering in his head. A shadow ran past him, charging down the hallway. Then another and still another. They were dirty and dressed in rags, full of rage and determination. Soon, there were hordes of them, jamming the hallway, all fighting each other to win their prize. Dager yelled for Casillya, but no sound came out. He plunged into the mass, fighting his way forward. He felt his arms being pulled apart and fingernails ripping at his flesh. He must stop them, but how? *They cannot get to her first. They must not.* But he felt himself falling to the floor, the stampede of hundreds trampling over his broken body. He tried to reach out, to stop them but he couldn't move. He was paralyzed. Somewhere, far into the distance, he heard her scream.

Dager Green winced in pain as a slit of light stabbed through a crack and burned into his eyes. As luck would have it, the cubby hole he had taken refuge in was not completely secluded from the outside world. Two of the wooden boards above left just enough space for the light to get in. Not only that, the light was not the normal dull gloom that radiated throughout the city. It was painfully bright, causing tears to stream down from his eyes. The light faded away just as he put his arm out to block the painful rays. It could only mean a hole had formed in the cloud layer just long enough to inflict its punishment upon him. It was rare that any of the direct sunlight got through, but it did happen. The irony was not lost on Dager. A rare breach in the cloud layer and it manages to find its way through the only opening in a hole where it stabs directly in his eyes.

It figures.

Dager staggered out of his hellhole refuge. He never wanted to come out. Each and every dark place that afforded a short sleep or reclusion became a private hideaway. He clung to those places for as long as possible until it seemed too dangerous to stay. He felt his own cowardice prevented him from staying in one place for very long. If he stayed, he might find a way out of this world, dying of starvation or perhaps from a beating by any number of the gangs that infested the city.

The skyline, what there was of it, offered nothing new to his tired eyes. The dark brown-yellowish haze hovered ominously over the entire city, slicing the view of skyscrapers two-thirds of the way up. The rumor was it drifted lower each year, making its way ever so slowly to eventually engulf everyone in a world without vision.

Dager wished it would come quicker. The chaos, filth, and crime mirrored the post-holocaust books of fiction from his youth. In some other lifetime, he could remember reading books of imagination transporting him to other worlds and to other possibilities. He would take them all into his head, eager for any flight of fantasy they might offer, just as long as they took him away from the real world for a while. How he wished for that real world now.

The world he presently faced was different than any of those works of fiction from his past. A deadly nuclear war of total devastation would have been preferable. There would have been no post-holocaust for the human race to try to survive in. There would have been no life at all, but peace prevailed. Peace among nations flourished, gently covering eyes with a veil of content while the inner cities corrupted themselves with uninhibited violence and confusion. When the order of things such as court systems and criminal confinement fell and martial law took effect, the disintegration of whatever was good in humans burned exponentially. The population, already overly immense in numbers, combined with filth and pollution to form an end result of poverty and disease. One particular disease arose from the fleeting breaths of mankind with the promise of final annihilation. The human race continued to survive, like hordes of cockroaches flourishing, fighting and breeding their way through existence.

It was not enough, however, for mankind to suffer though a crippling disease in the midst of a dark and horrible world. The ever-present drug concoctors stumbled upon an ingenious break-through and offered it upon the populous in the form of inhalants with the promise to reverse the ill effects of the poisoned atmosphere. The addiction came slowly at first, gently toying with both mental and physical states of being, and offering a newfound benevolence among people. At least, that was how it was in the first stage of addiction. It spread freely throughout the cities, giving all a short relief from their tired and dangerous existence. Then suddenly and inexplicably, it was gone from the streets. This accomplished an effect any drug dealer would kill for. The addicted society would do anything to have more. They would give anything and pay any price imaginable for just one more fix.

But it never returned. The strange euphoric release that sent an entire violent populous into a state of complete apathy was taken away like food ripped away from a starving man. What followed was mass confusion and hatred far beyond what existed before. The genetic-altering drug, or 'Blue Crystal' as it became known, soon revealed its true colors and produced horrifying side effects. The general population was scarred for life with physical mutations usually reserved for freaks of nature, giving everyone their own unique brand of defect. In an over-populated world, individuality now came at a very ugly price.

It might as well been a post-holocaust, war-torn

world. Only it happened a bit more slowly, taking intricate steps along the way to achieve the same result. The inhabitants were the unfortunate survivors and their children the inheritors of a world that nobody wanted. The world itself was a scarred relic of a once thriving people, its surface rising and falling with each decaying city. Giant, ominous steel structures, once man's claim of triumph and achievement, now descended into a long journey of death by neglect. Social growth had stopped or, more accurately, was receding at an alarming pace. Some form of dark-age barbarism awaited them now or, as Dager sometimes wondered, perhaps it was already here.

The street on either side was littered with vagrants. As Dager walked, one of them skipped a rock across his path, trying to hit him. It was a challenge to a fight. The instigator, most likely one with a death wish, was hoping Dager would turn and fight. Not even the gangs would fight the vagrants. They were the lowest inhabitants in the city, too cowardly to fight and far too weak to defend themselves. It was only those who made an effort to survive who made worthy opponents for the gangs. Those poor souls who still carried some small optimism for the world were the sworn enemies and eventual victims of gangs.

Dager stopped and turned to where the rock had come from. A skinny bald man with rotted teeth squinted back at him from twenty feet away. The man bobbed his head and gestured to Dager with curled fingers. He beckoned for a fight, taunting Dager with profanity and insults.

Dager ignored him and looked up the towering

wall of the giant building the vagrants were leaning against. Centered three floors up, a giant flat video screen droned on continuously. A perfectly groomed woman with no visible defects smiled out at the gloomy world below. Her non-porous face filled the screen, with deep blue eyes hypnotizing all who would behold her. It was the environmental report that came every hour, quarter past the hour.

"The Acromeda filtering station is working overtime for your health," she crooned. "Today, over 5 million cubic liters of air, purified to zero-point five microns will be spread into the atmosphere. The smog layer has lifted three centimeters in the past month alone by these efforts. The current Environmental Advisory Council estimate is complete eradication of the layer within a ten year period."

Dager looked up beyond the screen to the cloud layer in question. Every day they reported it was lifting, but every day Dager saw the same partial view of a broken window where the smog hovered. The brown haze floated like a sea of dirty cotton, casting its dark shadow over the entire city and beyond.

The pretty woman on the screen faded away to be replaced by the Officer of the First Order, Quintin Resarde. Skeletal bumps lay just under the skin on his scalp, making his face appear more like a skull. This was his defect and he wore it like a badge of courage. His eyes were pale blue and his face bore fierce determination. It was this man that emerged from the very dregs of society to blaze a path of righteousness and order for the chaotic and churning masses to follow. This man would solve the problems in the environment and find a cure for the genetic plague that threatened every newborn child. With firsthand experience of all the problems currently before man, he personally selected those who would seek out the solutions. He directed the efforts of scientists, physicians, and engineers all towards the common good of mankind. It was also true he was immediately responsible for the First Order Police that skimmed throughout the city on their armored cycles. He would admit this, turning a sad and disappointed eye to his followers as he explained how it was necessary to maintain some level of order among the chaotic environment and that he did not like this necessity at all, but it could not be helped. Indeed, it was the most disdainful of all his duties and his grandest of wishes that the violence levels would go down to a point where he could recall all of his troops.

However, this current broadcast was one seen periodically throughout the day, every day. With an infectious smile, he peered out into the world.

"My brothers, my sisters, my family," he started. "As you know from my previous announcements, our scientists have finally discovered a way to reverse the genetic defects that affect us all." The view shifted so the leader filled a small quarter of the screen and the form of a woman zoomed in to fill the rest. Her figure rotated to reveal complete perfection. As the leader continued, the figure was zoomed further so that only her head filled the space and rotated slowly. "Casillya is the product of the miraculous scientific breakthrough we have all been waiting and praying for. We continue our search for the group that abducted her from our facilities. We continue our search for Casillya herself. Without her, it is doubtful we will be able to duplicate our success. She is the key to our future. That is why the First Order has issued the following imperative: It is the duty and responsibility of each and every good citizen to report any and all information pertaining to Casillya or her abductors. To further that responsibility, it is crucial that every capable citizen use as much time and effort as possible to locate Casillya. The person or persons responsible for Casillya's recovery will be compensated by the Office of the First Order as follows…"

As the leader continued, Casillya's image reduced to a third of the screen and continued its rotation as new images filled the remaining space. The first of these images was of a man's mangled arm being genetically altered to be normal again. "They will be the first to receive genetic restructuring, once the process is completely perfected. They will receive a full dental and health package, with all incurred costs reimbursed at one hundred percent." An image of a young boy with no defects appeared. A dental hygienist buffed his gleaming teeth before he turned to the camera and smiled satisfactorily. "A complete compensation package which will take care of a lifetime of needs has been prepared for the individual or individuals responsible for returning Casillya to her home. And finally, habitation rights will be granted for citizenship in the newly constructed earth dome, *Nouvelle Terre*, due to be completed two years from now. Absolute clean air, freedom from violence and the pursuit of peace and tranquility await those who recover our lost lady of perfection."

The final images flashed glimpses of a domed paradise with a family of four breathing the air in deeply as bright rays of sunshine glinted over an abundance of plant life. Perfect people smiled at one another as they passed each other by in an uncrowded and peaceful little world. Then the image dissolved as Casillya's image was enlarged again and the leader's image appeared beside her.

"As you know," he continued in deep earnest, "Casillya can be identified by her perfection and can be verified by the symbol found on her wrist." With this, Casillya's head was replaced by a close-up of her wrist. The image was a simple one, the same symbol that adorned the buildings of the First Order, the same symbol Dager had seen in his dream: Rays of sunlight flowing to the earth. It was known as the 'rays of hope', adopted decades ago by the First Order, depicting a brighter future for everyone with the promise of abundant and free energy. The symbol was a perfect laser tattoo on a woman who otherwise had no identifiable marks -- no genetic defects, no birth marks, no remnants of childhood immunization and no fingerprints.

As the Officer of the First Order droned on about how the world was getting better every day, Dager found himself wishing he could hurl a rock far enough to hit the large view screen. He was on a personal mission, like so many others, to find Casillya. It was a thing to dream about in a world where dreams could not come true. Somewhere in the back of his mind, he admitted to himself that finding her was impossible and that searching was a useless venture. It was laughable that he, out of the thousands searching, would be the one to bring her in and claim the reward. But what else was there to do? And besides, there were those aiming to increase their chances by creating a loose network of searchers like himself. The pay was a meager amount of food, but it was something. Dager twisted his lips into a little sickening smile at the thought that he, Dager Green, may be everyone's last chance. If that was the case, he thought, the world was in for one hell of a disappointment.

Trash blew wildly across his path and suddenly a Zimmer flew past, nearly knocking him to the ground. Saddled upon it was a heavily armored enforcer of truth and justice for all. It seemed as if the Zimmer might burn all the vagrants, but his destination led him elsewhere and the cycle disappeared into the darkness. The First Order Police exemplified the government's ill attempt to maintain control. They cycled rampantly throughout the nation on their perpetually fueled death machines looking for anything appearing to contribute to the self-destruction of the world. Those appearances varied widely in the eyes of the First Order and they killed whatever they thought should be killed, causing suffering and chaos in their path of destruction. They were, in a large way, responsible for the continual downfall of society, the very thing they were supposed to be amending.

Dager ducked into the dark crevice of a skyscraper and walked while his eyes adjusted to the faint light inside. He kicked at the debris blocking his path. In another era, the lobby of this building might have been a thing of beauty, a welcome sight for travelers needing an expensive place to stay for the duration of their visit. Now, however, it was a war zone, vandalized to the hilt and littered with broken wood, concrete, and rusted metal. He trudged his way through the trash until he found the foot of the stairs. The building had no power. Even if there was, he was not so stupid as to take an elevator. The stairway would be a long haul, but a safer one. There were, however, the stair people. They met him at random steps and turns, coming out of the darkness, offering up anything their insane little minds could conjure for the chance that Dager might share a moment of peace with them. There was a chance that the encounter could get them killed, but they would accept that fate as well. In only the extreme cases did he have to physically push them out of the way. They became scarcer as he made his ascent.

The thirty-second floor greeted him with the first hints of strong daylight and started a stinging sensation in his eyes. He closed them and pressed on, giving them a chance to recover. He climbed blindly for a short time, using the handrail for guidance when suddenly, he felt a harsh thud on his back. Claw-like fingers gripped around his neck, strangling him. To Dager's advantage, the jumper was not very big or heavy. He hurled his body back against the wall and heard the attacker squeal in pain. The grip around his neck tightened even more. He went back and forth from wall to wall, smashing the parasite, causing the death grip to weaken each time. Finally, the small body slid down in defeat and tumbled down the stairs. A bloodied child of perhaps ten years came to rest at the turn of the stairs and lay motionless. Dager rubbed his neck and felt his own hot blood streaming from the scrape. He looked down the stairs at the child, his eyes tearing from the light. What had the kid hoped to gain? The only thing that might be of value would be food and no one was stupid enough to carry that around. It occurred to Dager as he winced at the lifeless body, that the kid probably got exactly what he was looking for.

Two more flights brought him to full daylight and he sat down for a moment to rest, feeling the agony of the piercing sunlight. Rags had been draped over the windows in an unsuccessful attempt to diffuse the sunlight.

Only six more floors to Dennison's abode, he thought. *Why did the Pig have to live up here in the daylight?*

Further upward, his eyes continued to water and he blinked more rapidly, trying to relieve the stinging pain. He was soon greeted by the first of the Pig's men on the floor just below his destination. The man quickly trained his weapon on Dager as he turned the corner. For a moment, the man looked like he might enjoy emptying his weapon into his new guest, but then he grunted and waved Dager forward. This guy knew of Dager's weekly meetings with the Pig, unlike the ones on the next floor. The Pig's right-hand men were always changing and these guys had never seen Dager before. As he put his foot on the last step, he was confronted by the Pig's top two cronies. They pointed the barrels of their weapons straight at Dager's head. They were both ugly. They were always ugly. One with skin grafted over one eye barked at the intruder.

"You've got two seconds, Perfect."

"Compared to you, anybody would look perfect," Dager said, rubbing his eyes.

They moved closer, pressing the buttons on their weapons that readied the explosive charge. The quick whine of the power build-up was something that one only wanted to hear if they were ready to die. These were the same weapons the First Order Police used to terrorize vagrants. As they skimmed by, it was not unusual to hear this sound, although louder and coming from a much larger gun, just before it sent a round ball of pure energy that plowed through its nearby victims. They called this the cleansing, the purification of the ills of society. Officially, they would report that gang violence erupted and as a last measure, when all other possible solutions had been explored, judgment had been made and punishment inflicted to eradicate the offenders. The truth was, however, just another member of the FOP was on a joy ride, testing the accuracy of his weapon and most likely bragging about how many vagrants he took down when he got back to home base. Most of the slayings were never reported.

"Alright, alright," Dager said, holding up his hands. "'The earth below is dark, the journey up is bright...'" It was the beginning of the pass phrase the Pig had given him to verify that he was allowed to enter. There was more to it, but he was having trouble remembering how it went.

"That's two months old, Perfect. You better think of something else quick."

Dager clenched his teeth. "It's two months old because I haven't been here in two months, you moron. Look, if I don't get this information to the Pig, it's gonna be on your head not mine."

The men didn't lift their weapons. Instead, the one with the bad eye pulled Dager forward then pushed him towards Dennison's lair. They forced their gun barrels into his back, and guided him through large double doors. Once inside, they gave him a final thrust causing him to stumble across a polished hard wood floor. Off to the far left, the Pig sat at a table stuffing his face with something. The commotion stopped his feast only long enough to recognize Dager's face and wave the men back outside.

Stacks of long, wooden boards were propped against the walls in the Pig's spacious penthouse, cluttering it even more than the stacks of unread books on the floor. Most of the ceiling was torn apart and the next two floors could be seen through a large gaping hole. The place was clean only in comparison to the world below. Otherwise, it was just another glorified rat-hole. Dager stood there with his eyes wet and body emitting a foul odor of sweat. The smell, however, was nothing compared to the stench that radiated from the Pig. Dager's stomach threatened to heave. He could not stand the site of the Pig, the only fat person he knew in the world.

Dennison was huge. He had long ago lost the ability to move on his own accord. He sat on a large, specially constructed chair that rolled him around and reclined to become his bed. As he ate, his jowls rolled as well as his ample chins -- a sweaty mass of loose flesh taking on a life of its own. Rolls of body fat protruded from inadequate clothing. Strangely enough, he had a small mouth that seemed to be crowded out by his flapping cheeks. His eyes were small, too. They were dark and gave him a sinister appearance, but it was the item in the middle of his face that gave him the nickname people only used behind his back. His nose looked exactly like a pig's. It was completely round and flat with two circular nostril holes. Dager also thought he heard him grunt like a pig on more than one occasion. Dennison 'the

Pig' was a lowly king among the dirty masses in his circles. He had achieved this status because he seemed to have an endless supply of food. Nobody knew where he got it or exactly how much he had, but everybody wanted their share of it. The only problem was, he was not exactly generous with his fortune.

Dennison stopped eating momentarily and began chopping something on an island counter as he spoke.

"Since your checking in at your normal time, I must assume you haven't found her." He didn't look up from his work.

"Not yet," Dager admitted. "But I know I'm getting closer."

"Getting closer," the Pig echoed sarcastically. "I have twenty other lookers out there and it's funny…because they all say the same thing. Why should I believe you?"

"Because I'm telling the truth," he lied. "I'm not stupid like the other lookers. I've been covering the city piece by piece, looking in every rat-hole there is. I'm looking in gang-turf, too. How many of your other lookers are doing that?"

"None that come back alive," the Pig chuckled. "All right, I'll keep feeding you for now, but remember this: I have people keeping tabs on my lookers. If I catch you out there hiding all day, I'll have one of my guys give you a brief tour of the roof. Very brief. You get my point?"

"I get it."

"Then go. The guy one floor down will give you instructions on where to pick up your next food package."

Dager turned to leave, but the Pig stopped him.

"Wait a minute. Here, try this. It's my latest

stuff". The Pig tossed something to the floor near Dager's feet. Bending down, he saw a couple of small green bits of food, which he picked up and tasted. Some sort of vegetable covered with butter. It was good.

"Green peppers. Dinner's gonna be tasty tonight." He grinned, showing off his white teeth with his little pig snout pointed upward.

In spite of his disgust, Dager smiled slightly at the pathetic excuse for a human in front of him, feeling part of his lip curve upward in its mutinous habit.

"Aren't you forgetting something?"

The Pig looked puzzled. "Huh? Oh…let me see. How about, 'dark skies, oh dark skies how I despise thee. Someday bright sunlight will your replacement be'."

Dager winced. "Can't you come up with something simple I can remember? Those goons out there nearly shot me when I got here."

The Pig shrugged. "You want more food, you'll remember it." With that, he went back to stuffing his face as if Dager had already gone.

After getting the instructions from Dennison's guy, Dager found his way to ground level and made it a point to walk a maze of building floors. Anyone following him would be thrown off his trail. A long abandoned garbage bin was the ultimate container of the food package. He shoved it into a hidden pouch in his pants and quickly walked away, altering his destination once again.

Dark buildings loomed overhead and the unmistakable feeling of peering eyes from every window raised Dager's guard. As he journeyed onward, the buildings became darker and smaller, the path more narrow. Eventually, the hard feeling of pavement beneath his feet was replaced by dirt. Permanent dwellings gave way to a shabby construction of huts. Dark and lonely houses developed from pieces of various wayward tin, wood, and steel pushed their way up through the dirt. If a tornado or even a strong wind passed through, all would be lost. Not that there was really anything to lose.

Before him now stood a small, shabby hut, thrown together with pieces of tin, wood and other scavenged materials, including a large sign from a long-forgotten goods store, hanging vertical for a door. The small, dirty face of a child peered cautiously at him from one of the many holes in the shack. It disappeared and quickly reappeared in another hole. This time it was smiling. He opened the makeshift door and another smiling face greeted him. This one belonged to a woman in her mid-thirties. Like everyone else, she was not immune to the toll that living in this world inflicted, but in her case the price was much higher. Rapid aging was the cruel joke her genetic defects were playing on her. She looked as if she might be in her late fifties. Her hair was unkempt and wrinkles were etched deeply around her eyes. The eyes, however, shone bright and seemed to be full of life when they looked at him.

"Each time you leave, I think that you won't be coming back," Sara said, putting her arms around him and kissing him.

"I think that too," Dager said. Her hands were already in his pouch, searching for whatever was there. She retrieved the food package and her eyes lit up. Chell, her little girl, ran up to him and hugged his leg, silent as ever.

"What have you brought us?" Sara inquired, tearing open the package. Then she frowned when she saw several small, plastic containers enclosed within. "Why do they do this?"

"Here." Dager withdrew a sharp blade and begin slicing the containers open, spilling them out onto the open paper. Chell ran up and grabbed a piece of food.

"Chell, wait! These have to be cooked," she scolded and grabbed the small piece of meat from her daughter's hand. "You want to die?"

"She'd be better off," Dager said and was met with glaring eyes. Sara was still pretty, even when she was angry, but she seemed to be aging faster with each passing day. Other than the rapid aging, though, she had hardly any other physical defects. Dager's own mutation did not show much on the surface. His legs were bulgy in some places and impossibly thin in others. People like that, those whose mutations were not immediately noticeable, were called 'Perfects'. Perfect men were always in danger of being killed while perfect women were always sought after for their sexual appeal. Dager knew that Sara was used by other men, but he maintained their loose relationship. It was that way with Perfects, keeping with their own kind just as the Uglys did. Other than brief companionship and the food, there was very little reason for him to visit. His mutations were not limited to his legs and prohibited any sensual relationship, so he and Sara remained celibate to each other. It was unusual in these times to maintain any kind of relationship. It was even more unusual for someone to share food. Yet, Dager managed to do both. Sometimes loneliness enveloped his soul and Sara seemed to take that pain away, at least for a little while. He felt that he was using her in this way. Perhaps that's why he brought them food.

Sara used Dager as well. It was nearly a year ago when he found Chell walking in the middle of no-man's land, picking up crumbs of dirt and tasting them for the possibility of food. Dennison had just recruited him for the mission and supplied him with a good amount of packages. When he happened upon the child, she fearlessly accepted a few bits of food from him, her facial expression seeming to consider the worthiness of the product. That was when Sara, in a surprise attack, ran at him like a wild animal and beat him with a steel bar. She almost killed him, but he was not so blessed. Chell came between the blows, causing her mother to stop in sudden horror and disbelief. Chell was motioning to her to stop and to drag the stranger into their home. It was the first time the child had ever communicated, even if it was only a crude sign language. Against her better judgment, Sara did exactly that. She treated his wounds the best she could and took his food packages. She prepared one of them and hid the others. It was almost two days before Dager could walk again. In that time, as Sara nursed him back to health, they had come to know one another. They slowly formed an unlikely trust relationship in an otherwise distrustful world.

Chell was different, though. She had trusted Dager from the beginning. She brought all her little broken toys to Dager to 'show off', as Sara put it.

Sometimes she brought him presents, too, like a group of small weeds that she considered flowers or an oddly shaped rock from outside. Her innocence and attention amazed Dager and he felt his heart soften for her. The child was not as lucky as her mother. Her forehead and brows were bulged from the defective DNA passed on to her. He attributed her lack of voice to trauma, ignorance, or genetic defect. Even with these faults, however, Dager could only see the face of a pretty child even from that first day. It was not just her physical appearance that Dager saw. Her determination to find a crumb of food coupled with her lack of fear and conceited judgment of his offering showed him a personality stronger than any that he had found. As if she were his own child, Dager was falling in love with her. As if such a thing was possible in these times.

Sara produced a huge meat cleaver and began cutting the small strips of food. More than once, she had used the cleaver in self-defense. It was a good thing she didn't have it during their first encounter, Dager mused, watching as she turned on the cooker and threw bits of the food pieces in a pan. As the cooker started to glow, he wondered what it would be like if they never achieved the perpetual power supply, the sun's energy beamed in tight microwave fashion to a number of stations on earth. Perhaps the world would not have survived this long. Perhaps they would have been better off.

"What do you do out there for so long?" Sara asked, her voice non-committal.

"You know what I'm doing. I'm looking for Casillya."

A chuckle came from her lips as she spoke. "She

doesn't exist, you know. She's a myth created by Mr. Perfect himself of the First Order."

"The Pig believes in her. The government wants to find her. They've got a lot of people looking. I figure she's out there somewhere or they wouldn't have so many looking for her."

She turned to him while prodding the frying pieces of food with a makeshift utensil. "What if they do find her? Is she going make us all perfect again?"

Dager sighed. "That's what they say. But I think it's too late for us. I think they want to make all the new babies perfect...start over, ya know?"

"A perfect baby," Sara smiled to herself, "wouldn't that be something to see." She suddenly realized what she said and turned to where her daughter was playing, just in time to see Chell's eyes fall. Sara turned back to the fryer, concentrating on it. "Of course, there's no such thing as a perfect baby anymore. We...we all have to be perfect in our own way."

"Oh, I almost forgot," Dager said, reaching deep into his pocket. "This is for you, Chell."

She walked to him, her eyes inspecting the object with doubtful consideration. It was a square piece of plastic that opened up like a book. Dager was sure it must have been some sort of toy when it worked. Pieces were missing or maybe it was broken, but he knew Chell would find meaning in it. She smiled her half-crooked smile at him and left for her corner to play with it.

Sara looked after her and then back to Dager. "She really loves you, ya know."

"Yeah," Dager said with a grim smile. He sat down on the floor and leaned up against the wall of the hut, slowly closed his eyes and rested.

It was some sort of a large warehouse. Garbage littered the floor like a dumping ground and the glass windows on either side were smashed. Dull daylight protruded from them, slightly illuminating the desolation. Large, broken crates and obliterated furniture were scattered sporadically about the place. Dager pilfered among the ruins for anything of value when he heard a noise. A shadow disappeared quickly behind one of the large objects.

I'm on someone's turf, he thought. *No doubt the crates make pretty good houses.*

He peered hard into the half-light, looking for movements while backing up slowly. A quick tap came from somewhere behind him. Then another from the left. He turned quickly, only catching brief glimpses of shadowy movement.

A set up.

From somewhere above, a figure came to land hard on top of a crate about twenty feet away. He was skinny with curly, dirty blond hair. He stood stout with arms at his hips and sharp, squinting eyes accenting a menacing smile. His heavy military boots looked almost new in contrast to the myriad of rags that clothed him. He had a cloth bag strapped over his shoulder full of something hidden from view and held a long metal rod that he used to steady himself on the crate.

"Come ta skiff a bit offa somemon else's trash pile, eh?" The man yelled across to him.

Dager could see figures emerging from the shadows on either side. *Gang Violents.*

"Didn't realize this was a claimed turf," Dager said, keeping a rough edge to his voice.

"Did ya ere that, Tommah? The begga didna know whose trash he wuz snoopin' roun in."

A large boy stood out with one arm distorted and raised. "Yeah. Whatcha say we teach 'em how much permission costs?"

Dager looked slowly around and counted at least nine of them. Some carried boards, others pieces of steel. Dager was pretty good at surviving on the streets. He had learned to fight tough at an early age, but this was no match. There was no reasoning with them. He was a dead man.

"Yeah, I was skiffing. But I didn't take anything. You guys can beat the hell out of me or I can bring you real food. It's up to you." There was his proposal. It was out there to be considered by the insane, and leveled with just enough indifference to show them he did not care if they killed him or not.

The leader on the crate laughed over-dramatically. "Ruh food? Ya gonna come in ere an dig through da gabage fer a bite, but ya gonna give us da ruh food?" He walked from one side of the crate to the other as if it was his personal stage, using his metal rod as a prop. "If ya got da ruh food, ya got a job and ain't no one got a job." He threw his arms up in exasperation. "How ya gonna give us da ruh food if ya ain't gotta job?"

Jeers flew up from the others, loudly agreeing with the logic of their leader.

Dager felt sweat run down his back and tried to hide his fear. "I've been hired by the government, but I'm not an enforcer. They pay me with food."

The lanky figure reached an arm over to one side

of his head and scratched beneath his deep curls. A bulge in the side of his head, his defect, became more apparent. He tapped his rod a couple of times on the crate, looking down as if disappointed. "Only two ugly jobs from da govament. Da killin' guys and da lookin' guys. Ya killin' o' ya lookin'?

"I'm looking."

He threw his head back as if had been hit with a knock down punch, grabbing the sides of his head and grimacing. "Lookin' fo Casillya? Da bitch da gonna save us all? Why dinya come out an' say in da furse place?"

"You know about her?"

"Evabody knows Casillya."   He spread out his hands, addressing the other members of the gang. "Da mutha o' da new human race. Ya know whut dey gonna do wid ah? Dey gonna stot a whole new wold wid ah. Wold full o' Puffics an' git rid ah all da Uglys. Wouldna dat be nice, Tommah?"

The big boy called Tommy laughed while slamming a makeshift club in his hand. "Yeah, it'd be real nice…for the Perfects."

The man on the crate started yelling quickly and angrily, making it even harder to understand his dialect. "Yeah, it'd be ruh nice fo da Puffics gettin' all da new blud an' all. Gettin' all puffict an' straight, but ya know whut da govament gonna do? Da govament gonna keep all da Puffics and kill da Uglys. Yeah, it'd be ruh nice fo da Puffics, but man ya mus hav da Blu Crysal in ya eyes. Ya mus be haf bline. Ya mine mus a gone an' lef ya 'cause look aroun ya, man." He spread his arms open to indicate the entire warehouse, his movements over exaggerated and theatrical. "Ya see any Puffics in ere?"

There was a clatter as his followers clanged their weapons around. Tommy said, "No, ain't none in here that we can see, Sketh."

The man with the steel rod thrust an arm out towards Tommy, acknowledging the statement. "See? I don tol ya. No Puffects in ere 'cause dis place…" He stopped suddenly and shook his head. "Tommah, Tommah, Tommah! How we gonna be so stupit? We mus be haf bline."

Tommy looked worried, as if being scolded. "What do you mean, Sketh? There ain't no…"

"Tommah!" The leader cried, "Open ya eyes and look around. Ain't no Puffects in ere, dis true…" He leveled his eyes on Dager. "Excep one."

Dager met his cold stare for a moment. Then he reached down and pulled a pant leg up to his knee, revealing one of his legs. It was thin as one of his arms, but bulged out in muscular masses in various spots all along the surface.

"Does this look perfect to you?" He said, angrily.

The man on the crate ignored Dager except for the return of a menacing smile. Then he tapped his rod methodically three times and the gang slowly closed in.

Dager came to slowly, all alone in a hard spot where a giant building and the street pavement met. In his mind, they were still there. Glimpses of imbeciles drubbing him to death with their crude weapons. Occasionally, as they turned him around, the brief vision of their leader came into his tortured view. Instinctively, he had put his arms up in defense, but there was no escape. He felt his body being pounded by pieces of wood and steel. The last thing he felt was a sharp blow to the head before his senses slipped away.

Now, he tried to move a little and an aching pain swept through his body. They usually killed their prey, gaining cheap surges of adrenaline and a false sense of superiority in their actions. His words had saved him, though. They knew he welcomed the end and they would not give him the satisfaction. It was better for them to bring him to the threshold of destruction, and then let him live...a fate worse than death. He could not even remember why he entered the warehouse as it was the perfect hideout for gang violents. He knew he might be killed when he went in there, so on some subconscious level, maybe he wanted to be killed. Yet, there was still a small part of him that must long for survival. It caused him to convey the only words that would save his life.

How he despised that part of himself.

He pulled himself up against a brick wall, moaning in pain. There was a thick fog hiding anything from sight. The night was upon him. Not that he could see anyway as his eyes were swollen shut. The temperature dropped quicker than the night before and he felt a chill run through his battered soul. He started out with a painful limp, not knowing where they had left him. This could be another city for all he knew, but it was doubtful. The same burning scent that filled his nostrils each and every day was there. The same sounds filled his ears. It was the sounds of the city, the sounds of the vagrants moaning and the far off screams of someone being tortured by a gang, maybe even the same gang that beat him to near death. The sounds all merged together to remind him he had not yet escaped this nightmarish world. It was the never ending cadence of the dying.

He stumbled along the walls of skyscrapers in a half-witted attempt to find his bearings. Wherever this was, it seemed unfamiliar to him. Dager Green, who had a picture perfect memory of nearly every crack and crevice within this prison of a city, was somehow lost. Groping helplessly for familiarity, he wondered how many others were wandering aimlessly among this God forsaken wasteland. His next move brought an unexpected change in the texture of the building. He could feel pieces of wood that were probably used to board up part of the wall. Suddenly, the wood gave way and he felt himself falling into the building. He heard the loud cracking noise of wood breaking around him. He was falling downward now, below street level. He expected to hit the ground quickly, but kept falling. He hit a wooden floor hard, but it did not stop there. The floor gave way, causing a loud crash with debris following him down. When he finally hit bottom, he felt something sharp stab into his side. This new pain added itself to Dager's existing collection of torment and unconsciousness found him once more.

In another, much cleaner part of the city, the *Office of the First Order* building jutted into the sky like a majestic monument. The main building was positioned in the center of the complex, adjacent to Acromeda station which was the main filtering station as well as the hub of the power grid. The center building was a beautiful accomplishment of architecture in a world where such artistic attempts were no longer made. Its round base curved upward into the sky and then blossomed outward forming a huge mushroom shape, just under the cloud cover. Around the base of the mushroom, hundreds of dome covered pads shot out at random lengths. These were used for meeting areas, cafeterias, recreation and, in some cases, homes for high officials. A few of the pads were not covered at all, serving as heliports. Two circular bands crisscrossed the entire mushroom, providing quick access to the outer dome areas. Within them, horizontal elevators raced along their path, giving occupants a full view of the world below. The entire complex was more like a city within a city.

Originally, the complex housed the most brilliant minds on the planet. It was a scientific community, built in tribute to the golden mantra sought after for ages: perpetual power -- free and clean energy for all in a world nearly exhausted of all other natural resources. But when the old government fell at the hands of revolutionaries -- a network of freedom fighters claiming that everyone's last few liberties were being systematically ripped from the people -- a new order emerged. The new order, led by revolutionary Quintin Resarde and his personal troops, stormed the complex and claimed it as headquarters for a new government of freedom. The scientist population, already haggard and worn by attacks from gangs, the addition of vagrants in the community, and the confusion that martial law had brought, could only step aside as Resarde and his men moved in and began cleaning house. He kept most of the scientific community, eradicated the gangs and forced the vagrants out of the boundaries of the complex.

Resarde proved himself an unlikely hero to most, a feared overzealous radical to others. He and his followers dealt the final blow to the politicians and a government that had led its people down a path of self-destructive totalitarianism, only thinly disguised as a protective world power looking after the needs of its people. Slowly and methodically, individual freedoms were replaced by laws and regulations aimed at protecting citizens from themselves. Instead of bolstering education and moral responsibility, government attempted to ease the symptoms of an increasingly decadent society by trying to curtail deviant behavior. By pumping out increasingly stringent laws, budgeting greater law enforcement and building endless prisons, the government gave birth to a monstrous breeding ground of criminals, an assembly line of sociopaths, murderers and gang upheavals, marking the end of any moral beliefs and common decency.

Resarde brought down the government by shifting the balance of power and by turning the people against it. He communicated his ideas through an information network, citing countless examples of how the government system had gone astray, leaving in its wake a lost people that must find its way again. He became a cult hero almost overnight, a faceless vigilante that would stand up for the true freedoms and rights of the people. Resarde proclaimed that he was not one to sit back and argue about wrongs of government and society like so many media commentators before him. The time for talk was over. Now was the time for action. Now was the time for those in power to answer to the people for their actions, for their crimes and dishonesty. He made it clear that he did not advocate violence against his fellow man, but that all must rise up and prepare for change.

There were many that thought Resarde needed to be arrested or locked away in an asylum, but there were many more that saw the truth in what he had to say. His words struck a chord in the hearts and minds of the public. Resarde's charismatic voice fueled them on and soon networks began to spring up everywhere, ready to fight for Resarde's cause. The Resarde Resistance was born and, through a secret network of communication, the followers took up peaceful protest on key issues across the nation. The resistance grew to such an overwhelming size, that it actually started to work. The people could no longer be ignored because they were the majority. What at first was viewed as a handful of radicals had become a movement unlike anything in the nation's history. The resistance gained its first victory in getting the law of national identification overturned. No longer would people need to be implanted with a mandatory identification chip. It would take years for the infrastructure of the nation to implement the change, now having to rely on methods used in the past, but it was seen by Resarde and his followers to be the turning point. They could effect change and they could make a difference. Suddenly, those who had regarded Resarde as a radical now began to look at him as a proponent for justice, someone who would stand up for the people when no one else wanted the job.

For Resarde, however, the change was not coming

fast enough. The government was a painfully slow behemoth that acted like a reluctant political mule. Nor did he trust the changes being made would ever see the light of day. Those in power could simply be pacifying an angry populous, admitting to the public that changes needed to be made, but all the while intending to circumvent their own newly created laws.

Resarde soon made plans to take actions of a much less peaceful nature. Some of his followers, however, were far ahead of him. Some leaders of different sects attacked key areas, proclaiming the Resarde Resistance revolution had begun. Other Resarde Resistance leaders thought they somehow missed out on the action and initiated violent protests of their own. Resarde began losing control of his network. He demanded that no protest of any kind take place without his approval, but it was too late. The Resistance already controlled most of the public and these actions were seen as being the next step in Resarde's plan. Hordes of people rushed to join the Resistance. They could see the beginnings of a revolutionary war and they wanted to be on Resarde's side. Those turned away began forming their own sects in the name of Resarde and the resistance groups multiplied, often emerging with zealot leaders with their own agendas.

Resarde watched as his network spun out of control with random acts of violence multiplying and a government fighting to maintain control. Soon, martial law was put into effect. Every action the Resistance took was attributed to Resarde himself, whether he condoned it or not. Some, however, began doubting Resarde was behind any of the schemes, having not been heard from in months. Resarde began to believe there was no other way for this to happen and that any form of revolution could not be completely controlled. However, he was outraged he had no control over the events that were taking place. It was time to end it and to bring a balance back to society. As it was, there would be revolutionaries cropping up everywhere to claim power, maybe even an ambitious rival would emerge claiming that he was Resarde himself. That simply would not do.

Resarde collected all the members of his personal regime together and called upon a few of those remote leaders still loyal and in contact. He gathered a small army. Somehow, news of this new coalition leaked to the government and the element of surprise was no longer his. Government defense measures were taken to protect key facilities and officials while troops were sent out to take out Resarde. What they had not counted on, however, was Resarde's cunning ability as a tactician. He purposely leaked false information on the location of his training camp. At the same time, he left bogus indications of when and where his first attack would take place. With government troops concentrated as far away from his real target as possible, Resarde made his move. The scientific complex never knew what hit them. He took the existing defense force by surprise, but half of them were Resarde supporters anyway. The take-over was quick and mostly painless for the shocked scientific community. Resarde hand-picked those who would stay, keeping mainly the top scientists and the grunt workers keeping the station running. The rest were told they could leave one of two ways:

peacefully or by force. Only a handful had to be pushed out by force, claiming they would not vacate their homes. It only took the forceful removal of one of the families and the remaining resistors fled quickly, none of them accustomed to dealing with violence.

Resarde now controlled the most powerful place on Earth. Not only did he have the brightest minds on the planet at his disposal, he had Acromeda station, the main hub of the microwave collecting stations. The station drew a staggering seventy-five percent of the continent's power from feed relay satellites in space. When he made his first broadcast from the complex, he stunned the world. All the propaganda spread about him for the past year had fashioned an image of someone who would take the government by force, a hostile take-over leading him to political power. Now Resarde, in essence, did have the political power. With key scientists and Acromeda station under his control, he literally had the power to bring the government to its knees.

He expected a long battle, an exhausting game of chess where he would need to counter government attempts to regain control of the station. What he did not count on was what happened next. The Resistance factions, upon hearing the news that Resarde had resurfaced with this mind-blowing stunt, propelled into action against the existing government. Over a quarter of governmental defense personnel defected to the Resistance and sabotaged operations from the inside. The political infrastructure began crumbling when some politicians, fearing for their lives and the lives of their families, completely abandoned office. The coming months were among the bloodiest in history with Resistance groups attacking and destroying at any given time with little or no regard to human life. Suicide bombers began emerging, taking out single key targets one at a time. The influx of new recruits to the Resistance grew exponentially while government forces only became weaker.

All the while Resarde watched in amazement from his office high within the complex as the events unfolded. Positive it would all be over soon, he began drawing up plans for the First Order, a government based on directives rather than laws and regulations. The underlying purpose of the First Order was to solve the problems facing society today. Among the top initiatives were to eradicate hunger, raise the quality of life, remove the genetic problem, abolish the violent gangs, provide housing and shelter and raise the general intelligence level of the people. By the time the revolution was over, Resarde was ready to unveil his plan to a population starved for direction and a new purpose.

All this happened over two years ago. Now Resarde stood in his office gazing out at the broken city horizon, an eye-sore of vagrant infested architecture blanketed by the ugly brownish haze. At times, he wished the smog layer was low enough so it would cover the entire landscape.

The entrance bell chimed twice. Resarde went to his desk and opened the entrance to his office with a button. Resarde's right-hand man, General Samuel Korg, stood at parade rest in the opening. Resarde motioned him in and went to his side bar to pour a drink. Korg stood over two meters tall with a muscular frame. When they first met, Korg was a gung-ho ex-military munitions expert. While in the service, he barely made it above Sergeant before receiving dishonorable discharge for misconduct. Korg was a loose cannon, but he had been eager for a cause and Resarde offered him one that he believed in. Resarde brought him into the inner circle and made him General of his band of troops. When things escalated to violence, Korg led the men according to Resarde's wishes and had the scars to prove it. These days, however, Korg presided over the First Order Police, becoming more of an administrator than a man of action. Korg excelled at few things and administration was not one of them. Resarde heard more and more reports indicating Korg was reverting to his old military ways. Except now, instead of a string of misconducts, when Korg lost his temper, one of his subordinates might be found dead a few days later. Resarde knew exactly what Korg needed.

"Drink?" Resarde offered.

"No, thank you, sir," Korg said. After entering the room, he had resumed his military stance.

"Good Lord, Sam, relax," Resarde demanded. "We've known each other for years and you still treat me like a commanding officer."

Korg made an uncomfortable attempt to loosen up. "I never let my guard down, even in friendly company. It keeps me sharp."

"Right," Resarde said, dismissing it with a drink. He hesitated before speaking again. "How long have we been searching for our girl, Sam?"

"I don't know, sir. Almost a year, I guess."

"Almost a year," Resarde echoed. "Eleven months and sixteen days. We've got the entire population out hunting her down and your troops scouring the city day after day and yet we've turned up nothing. I think it's time that we face the fact that she is probably dead."

Korg was shocked. "Sir? That can't be. Someone would have found her body at least…reported it."

"Or maybe there was no body to report. Did you ever stop to think that maybe one of your elite squad might have vaporized her in one of their cleansing runs?"

Korg stiffened. "Not possible, sir. At that range, she would have come up on the scanners. She's still out there somewhere."

"Perhaps," Resarde said. "But this has gone on long enough. I want her found, whether she is dead or alive. That is why —" He took another drink and placed the glass flatly on his desk "—I'm personally assigning you the task of finding her."

Korg cocked his head, confused. "I don't understand, sir. I already have the responsibility of finding her. My division is—"

"You're division hasn't made the slightest bit of progress the entire time she's been missing! I want you to go out and find her. Bring a small team if you want to, I don't care. Just find her, dead or alive. All we need is a bloody strand of her hair, for God sake. But we need proof it is her, so you best bring me back more than a piece of hair."

"But what about my FOP responsibilities?"

"I've already made arrangements for Benahr to temporarily take over as head of your division."

"Jim Benahr?" Korg asked, incredulous. "He will drive the division into the ground in two weeks! Besides, what makes you think that one man can find her when we've got thousands out there looking now?"

"General," Resarde said slowly, his patience stretched, "I have the utmost confidence in you. I've always been able to count on you to get the job done and for whatever reason, you seem to work best alone. You know what's at stake here. Now, go out there and get me her damn DNA!"

Korg's jaw was set. "And if I can't find her?"

Resarde shrugged. "Then you best not come back."

General Korg's eyes widened a bit. Then he straightened, turned on his heel and left.

Something soft wiped cool water across Dager's face. As his blurry eyes tried to focus, a vague figure hovering over him came into view. His first instinct was to jump up and protect himself from whatever strange situation lay before him, but he felt tired and battered and really did not care if danger was at hand or not. Death was becoming a thing to be longed for where once it was feared.

Dager thought he heard music playing softly in the distant background. He thought he heard the sound of violins and a deep, soothing cello. No doubt, he was either dead or dreaming. He also heard the unmistakable sound of water running carelessly, but interrupted momentarily when something obstructed its path. Then soft hands brought water to his face again, pouring it generously upon him and then concentrating the rest to his mouth. Dager did not fight it. He did not care if it poisoned his wretched body, but the drink was not accompanied by the familiar bitter taste and slimy texture. It tasted...much like it had in the old days.

"Slowly, slowly," a gentle voice sang. "Not all at once."

Dager forced his eyes into focus now, needing to see who it stood before him. Gradually, her form sharpened. Hazy and blurry outlines merged together to present an accurate view and Dager could not believe his eyes. Kneeling beside him and tending to his wounds was the most beautiful and perfect women Dager had ever seen. There were photos from years ago. Glamorous images of impossibly beautiful women that had become collector's items of the rich. Even if they were alive, here and now and combined in their beauty, they would not match her perfection. Yes, her hair was tossed and her cloths rags, but her face was radiant and her eyes were alive in these dead times. At first wondering what her defect was, Dager began to wonder if she had a defect at all. Was she, as she seemed to be, completely perfect?

Her hands moved over his face again. Dager grabbed her arm tightly and raised it so that he could focus on her wrist. Dager blinked several times, wanting to be sure that the design was really there. It was.

"Yes, it is true," she said slowly, "I am Casillya. Not quite what you expected am I?"

"I...," his voice trailed off, at a loss for words. His search led him to almost every hole in the city with only rumors to go on. How many packs of lookers the government hired, he had no idea, but he was sure there were quite a few. If she were real, if she were to be found at all, he had always doubted it would be him that discovered her. To stumble in blindly, to literally fall right into her hands was beyond his scope of reality. Yet, here he was with her.

"It is all true, everything they told you," she explained. "I am the product of a genetic success. The project that began in an effort to re-introduce normal DNA into our defective society achieved its goal."

Casillya dampened the cloth again and covered its surface with some sort of sterile solution before applying it to his grotesque legs. Her perfect beauty contrasted with his ugliness and it gave him a feeling of shame. He felt he did not belong near her.

"What they probably did not tell you is that I had five sisters," she continued, stinging his legs with her healing cloth. "Five twins all like me. Can you imagine that? I am the only one still living, though. Whatever they did different with me allowed me to survive. It also made me *want* to survive."

With some effort, Dager sat up on his elbow and looked at his surroundings. The place was mostly dark and looked as if it had been burned at some point. The memory of his tortured beating and subsequent fall into oblivion came back to him now. He suddenly looked down at his side where something had stabbed him during the fall. The area was now clean and bandaged.

"So you escaped," he said. "You found a way out."

She laughed genuinely. Even that brought a sort of perfection to his ears, perhaps because it was unheard of in these times. "It was not hard to leave. It was the last thing they thought I would do or would even be capable of doing." Suddenly, her eyes became weary and old. "But I'm so tired of hiding...of trying to stay ahead of all of you. I know you've been looking for me, seeking me out and waiting for me to make a mistake. I'm tired of playing this game."

Casillya brought the cloth over her water drain and wrenched it out for the last time. She turned to him again, her beautiful amber eyes piercing his soul with her honesty. "I'll go back with you."

A dust storm eroded the city. The seasons were changing hands again and Dager and Casillya were caught in the middle of it. Somehow, Dager managed to guide them to Sara's place, hoping for a brief rest before continuing on.

They stood inside near the door, unwrapping the gritty rags that clung to their bodies. Casillya had much more to remove. Dager had covered her well, intending to protect her from more than just the storm. She looked more like a stocky man than female and, as she peeled off the disguise, Sara met them with alerted eyes. Chell looked on, a suspicious and superior expression covering her face. When Casillya finally removed the last veil from her face, Sara brought a trembling hand to her lips in disbelief.

"You've found her," she said in a broken voice. "God save us all, why did you bring her here?"

Dager did not answer as he took the bulk of rags and stuffed them into a nearby cubbyhole, out of the way. Chell took to Casillya immediately. With an innocent smile, she walked up to this new stranger and led her by the hand to a small collection of toys. Silently, but with the same inviting smile, she brought out various play things for the approval of her guest.

Amazingly, Casillya sat down on the floor with her and joined in the imaginary play as if she were visiting a childhood friend.

Sara and Dager sat together at the large, round container turned on end which served as a table.

"We needed rest and shelter from the storm," Dager explained apologetically. "I didn't want to stop anyplace else. It would be too dangerous."

"Look at her. It's true. She's perfect," Sara said, her eyes fixed on the visitor.

"Yeah," Dager agreed, "she's real. I was beginning to wonder..."

The terror came back into her eyes when she looked at him. "She'll be the death of us all. Can't you see that? Do you know what you're doing?"

"I know exactly what I'm doing."

They looked on as Casillya and Chell played together. Chell turned her head quickly from one toy to the next, pulling them into her imaginary world. Dager wondered where her world was and wished he, too, could go there. Even Casillya, easily relating to Chell's creative play, was denied entrance to her peaceful content.

As Dager watched, he saw Chell pause for a moment when she handed Casillya the square piece of plastic that he had given to her. Her innocent, round eyes looked up at her new friend with wonder. She lifted her hand and softly touched Casillya's cheek. Dager saw her lips move in an uncharacteristic way.

"Pretty," she said. The word had come out slow and soft. Then she continued playing.

Sara put her hand over her mouth and tears streamed down her cheeks. Dager felt something in his heart, but was not sure what it was. It was the first time anything in this world had touched him so.

Dager journeyed up the high rise to Dennison's abode two days before his next scheduled appointment. His buddies tried to turn him back but Dager insisted the Pig would want to see him. The main grunt grew irritated and armed his weapon, ready to blow him back down the stairs. The Pig appeared at his door and halted the misunderstanding. He ushered him quickly inside and moved back to his corner. His stubby hands fidgeted with some broken electronic device.

He was ecstatic at this early arrival, edging his snout to and fro, beckoning Dager for information. "What do you have for me? Get your hands on some good information, did ya?"

"I found her."

Dennison stopped and stared. Slobber formed around his open mouth and he shook his head, causing his jowls to roll back and forth. "You w-w-what?"

"I said I found her. Are you deaf?" Dager felt his teeth clenching. The thought of the Pig getting rewarded in any way made him feel sick.

"Well, where is she? You got her in hiding? That's good, but it's too dangerous. You have to bring her to me. Cover her up good and bring her to me."

"Oh, I brought her to you," Dager told him evenly.

A look of confusion masked the Pig's face and he wrinkled his snout.

Dager reached into his pouch. "At least I brought part of her."

"What the..."

Dager withdrew part of Casillya's arm and hurled it at the pig. It hit him in the chest and fell to the floor, the symbol on the wrist clearly visible. Rays of hope.

The Pig looked down at it, horrified. Then his face became a bright red and he glared at Dager. "What in God's name have you done to her? They wanted her whole. They wanted her alive."

"Well, now nobody's perfect, are they?"

The Pig heaved himself out of his mobile chair and fell to his knees with arms outstretched towards the appendage of his prize. For a short time, he was lost and his angry face became a mixture of anguish and disbelief. Dager knew in an instance the Pig would have him killed. He slipped out quickly and from a distance, heard Dennison squeal out the desperate orders.

When Dager returned to Sara's place, Casillya was there waiting and ready to go. It was not like she had much to carry along for the trip. Her face wore an expression of somber expectation. She was used to being on the run, of always having to move somewhere. Now, however, she had nothing to run from. The First Order would have their precious DNA samples or whatever it was they needed. That is, unless the Pig was right and they did need her whole. In that case, they would have to do without. She did not have to come with him, but she didn't want to be alone anymore.

Sara looked at him with a grim smile. She knew that this was goodbye. She and Chell would stay behind, living the only life they knew and would go on with their own struggles.

Dager saw in her eyes now a sadness, a longing for different times where they could have created together the sort of dream they never dared imagine. Some other place, some other time. He went to her and they embraced tightly, both realizing they cared more for each other than they ever could admit.

Up to now, Chell was full of energy, jumping up and down and eager to go out into the world on a trip to some place far away, to some place much better than this. Even though her imaginary play world gave her comfort from reality, she was caught up in the inevitable process of growing older. It would become harder and harder for her to escape from the world. Now, she looked up at Dager with a finger bent between her lips. A certain look of tragic uncertainty shown in her eyes as she saw her mother's tears. Dager knelt down and spoke softly to her for a moment. He needed to tell her that she had to take care of her mother now and that she had to be strong. He explained to her she need not be afraid to use her voice anymore. Perhaps if more people learned to use their voice, they could find a way out of this condemned fog. He wanted to promise her he would see her again, but could not bring himself to do it. There was always something about her that demanded honesty and would not allow even a small exaggeration of the truth. It was hard for him to admit a feeling so rare and absurd in these times, but he hugged her close and told her that he loved her.

The two travelers were greeted by another sandstorm. Although it would make for a rough journey, Dager knew it was ultimately to their advantage, shielding them from detection. They left from the shambles of the makeshift dwellings and continued until they felt the pavement of the city under their feet. Soon that, too, would be gone and they would be in unknown territory, neither of them knowing where they were going or what they would find. The only thing they knew for certain is that they would not be alone.

Author's note: I've never been a big fan of post-apocalyptic science fiction. I can only guess that the reason I decided to write this story, which dives head-first into an extremely dark post-apocalyptic world, is to challenge myself and my writing. Stepping out of my comfort zone seems to be a reoccurring theme in my writing, which I guess is a good thing.

This story, originally titled "In the Real World" after a Roy Orbison song, was written in the first-person, but later changed to third person as I developed a novel outline for it. In the (unwritten) novel version, the main character is more of an unlikely action hero and of course we learn more specific details as to why the world is the way it is and of the government's true evil nature with its sinister leader. Still, I think this short story holds up nicely and we are able to get a clear picture of a world gone astray.

Somewhere along the line, I thought it might impress a potential publisher if I obtained the rights to include some of the lyrics from the Roy Orbison song. However, that idea was scrapped once I contacted the music publisher and found out how much it would cost to obtain permission to use the lyrics. I was then left with a scene where the main character hears 'Orbison's wonderfully melodic alto somewhere in the background'. Later, with the title of the story changed and while doing a rewrite, I realized it didn't make much sense to include the Orbison reference. It just didn't fit. It's amazing how often you can fall in love with an idea and fight so hard to hold onto it, until you finally give in to the realization that it just doesn't play well with the rest of the world you have built around it. Still, it's nice that the original inspiration started the seed growing.

ABOUT THE AUTHOR

D.V. Nobles has always enjoyed using the creative side of his brain. From an early age, he began writing short stories and put together his own comic books. Later, he discovered the world of music and began writing, playing and producing his own songs as well as music by others. He has been involved in filmmaking, photography and various other artistic ventures. He also enjoys creating 3D models and is owner of blenderfornoobs.com, which offers free tutorials on the Blender 3D software.

Other books by D.V. Nobles (available on Amazon.com):

Imperfect Strangers
Journey into the Unknown – The Mystery of the Out of Body Experience

www.ingramcontent.com/pod-product-compliance
Lightning Source LLC
Chambersburg PA
CBHW050039180626
46810CB00002B/809